D1422675

THE DEVIL'S MILL

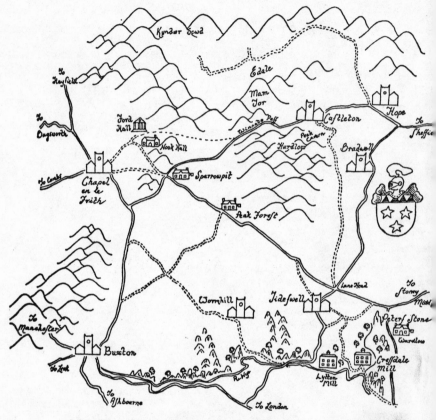

Map illustrating the Travels of Master Jeremy Ollershaw

THE DEVIL'S MILL

by

WALTER UNSWORTH

CICERONE PRESS
MILNTHORPE, CUMBRIA

© Walt Unsworth 1968
First published by Victor Gollancz Ltd 1968
Reprinted 1970, 1973
This edition published by Cicerone Press 1989

ISBN 1 85284 045 5 (Hardback)
ISBN 1 85284 043 9 (Paperback)

Text printed and bound by Butler & Tanner Ltd.,
Frome, Somerset, England

And did the Countenance Divine
Shine forth upon our clouded hills?
And was Jerusalem builded here
Among those dark Satanic mills?

BLAKE

CONTENTS

CHAPTER ONE

WINNATS PASS

THOUGH IT WAS scarcely five o'clock, the December evening had fallen swiftly over the Derbyshire landscape and already a moon had risen bathing the moors in a ghostly glow. Snow had fallen an hour or two before so that the undulating landscape lay under a white mantle, reflecting the moonbeams in such a way that a man could see for miles, as though it was broad daylight.

Only the ribbon of road showed black against the surrounding hills, winding its tortuous way from Chapel en le Frith past the old cross-roads inn at Sparrowpit to the Winnats Pass and Castleton.

On the road a small coach, pulled by a pair of roan mares, toiled against the incline, its wheels now jolting in the frozen ruts, now skidding on the patches of black ice where puddles had frozen in the grip of the night air. It was hard work for the horses and the steam rising from their flanks was plainly visible to the coach driver, huddled over his reins.

From time to time the driver stirred himself to flick the reins as if to encourage his charges to greater efforts, though without much success. He was cold, despite his thick top-coat turned up round his face, and his gloves, but he consoled himself with the thought that if God and the road were willing they should reach the inn at Castleton within the hour. The prospect of a good supper and a mug of spiced ale before the inn fire cheered him immensely against the cold.

1*

Inside the coach sat a woman and a boy, both well wrapped against the rigours of their journey for it was scarcely warmer inside the vehicle than out. She was a woman of about fifty, plump and with a kind, motherly face which every so often smiled encouragement at her young companion as if to comfort him against the cold and the incessant jogging of the coach.

For his own part the boy seemed to be taking the journey well. He was a robust youth of about fourteen, with a striking dark face like one who has spent his childhood in sunnier climes than bleak Derbyshire and a crop of black hair which curled down the nape of his neck in an unruly fashion giving his handsome features a look which betrayed his ancestry. That he was a Celt—Irish or Welsh —was unmistakable, though when he spoke his voice had no trace of accent.

'The horses seem to be slowing ma'am,' he said to the woman.

She smiled, then replied, ' 'Tis a steep brew and no doubt Jacob is having a hard time driving them. We passed the crossroads a little way back and 'tis a mighty pull up to the top of the Pass.'

'Tell me about the Pass,' the boy requested.

'Local people call it Win Yats,' she replied, 'and there's those as say 'tis the work of the Devil. 'Tis like a gorge carved through the mountains with fearful cliffs on either hand and superstitious folk say that Old Nick was so jealous when he saw the beautiful way in which God had fashioned Derbyshire that he took his sword and tried to destroy it. The Winnats, they say, is a slash from the Devil's sword.'

'It sounds a fearsome place,' said the boy shuddering involuntarily.

'Aye, 'tis fearsome right enough. The cliffs are so tall that on some days the sun never shines in the Pass. Beyond it there lies a great mountain the like of which is not to be found anywhere else, for it visibly shakes and shivers as though still quaking from the Devil's sword-blow. The locals call it Mam Tor, meaning Mother Mountain, for all the bits and pieces it shakes off roll down its great cliffs to form a huge pile of stones, for all the world like an infant mountain, and 'tis as though the one was giving birth to the other.'

'What a strange land this is!' the boy exclaimed.

'Strange indeed. A voyager might travel far before he meets a land like Derbyshire.'

'Then there are other wonders?'

'At the far end of the Pass, on a high crag stands the old castle of the Peverils who were once Lords of the Manor, though they've been gone many a long year. Beneath the castle, however, is a cave which some say is the largest in the world and in the cave live a whole village of strange subterranean folk, only half human.'

The boy shuddered again at this, then fell silent to brood on the mysteries of this unusual land. The only sound was the creaking of the carriage wheels in the icy ruts and an occasional curse from Jacob as he urged the horses to greater effort.

The moors which had been open and rolling gradually began to assume a sterner aspect as the little coach wound its way into a narrow vale. Away in the distance Rushup Edge could be seen flinging its great height at the night sky, whilst nearer to hand the conical shape of Eldon Hill towered over the road like some enormous sugar loaf. The road climbed steadily all the while, not permitting the horses any relief from their long struggle.

Perched on his driving seat the cold and hungry Jacob regarded the way ahead with some misgivings. Before it plunged into the Winnats gorge, the road crossed a high saddle and he could see that storm clouds were fore-gathering there as though the mountains were intent on making their own weather. To cross Winnats at night was bad enough, Jacob reflected, but to cross it in a storm was twice as bad.

Still, there could be no turning back; the inns at Chapel en le Frith were full, and the only other shelter was in Castleton. Storm or no storm, the pass had to be crossed.

The threatened storm held off until the coach had breasted the last rise and begun its descent towards the gorge. At first it was a mere flurry of snow, but within minutes the flakes fell in earnest, obliterating everything in a blinding white curtain. The two mares, at last re-leased of upwards toil, cantered downhill at a spanking pace, whilst Jacob, driving blind, held on to the reins with all his might.

Suddenly, lightning flashed, turning the sky and the swirling snow a vivid lilac, and hard on the lightning came a crash of thunder which seemed to shake the very hills themselves. The horses, already unnerved by the blinding snow, reared and snorted in sudden terror, and Jacob, caught unawares, was almost thrown from his seat. Hard on the first flash came another, then a third, very close, and the poor animals, frightened out of their wits, reared again, then bolted in panic down the steepen-ing, icy road.

Jacob fought the reins like a man possessed, but to no avail. The horses were crazed beyond human control. The coach lurched and swayed with increasing velocity. Inside, the two occupants were thrown to the floor by the first sudden charge, but so quickly did it happen that they had scarcely time to comprehend their plight.

Flash after flash of lightning lit the sky as the storm gathered to full fury. Each succeeding flash added to the terror of the crazy horses, spurring them in their mad flight. The coach rolled more and more crazily, skidding and sliding on the ice-rutted road, now cornering in a wild sideways swing, now dashing headlong downhill.

As the road plunged into Winnats the gradient steepened and too late did the horses realise that they were now beyond their own control. They were powerless to stop, carried forward by their own mad momentum. Inside, the two passengers were thrown violently from side to side, bruised and battered at every turn. They too were powerless, unable to help themselves in the chaos of the hurtling vehicle.

A luggage trunk, strapped to the outside of the coach, burst its bonds to go flying off and vanish in the snowstorm. Then, without warning, the two doors burst open and were immediately wrenched from their hinges by the rush of air. At the same time, the wheels hit a pothole in the road, causing the vehicle to jerk and swerve sideways. The boy, semi-conscious from the battering he had received on the floor of the coach, felt himself flung towards the open doorway. There was nothing he could do to stop himself—he scarcely realised what was happening—only that he was turning over and over as if in some terrible nightmare. Then a searing pain shot through his brain, coloured lights danced in his eyes, and he lost what little consciousness remained.

The coach, still sideways on, slid remorsely down the steep hill. At a bend it left the road to go crashing into a boulder, shuddered momentarily, then somersaulted into the wall of rock at the roadside. There was a sickening rending and splintering of wood. The demented horses, freed at last of their burden, dashed off into the night.

He awoke with a throbbing head and the taste of blood in his mouth. A sharp pain was stabbing him in the small of his back and when he summoned the energy to roll over he discovered that he was lying on a heap of broken rocks, the spoil from a crumbling limestone cliff which rose overhead like some enormous ship's sail. He felt sore all over, every little movement hurt, and he wondered what had happened and how he came to be lying in the open on a winter's night, with snow falling.

A drowsiness came over him, pleasant and comforting, but a kind of sixth sense warned him not to fall asleep; that the snow and the cold were certain death. He raised himself from his hard couch, first on to all fours like a dog, then, unsteadily, on to his feet. His first attempt was a failure; his legs turned to water and buckled beneath him sending him sprawling in the snow again. He cried aloud at the pain of it, but after a moment or two, tried again. This time he was successful, and half walking, half crawling, he stumbled over the rough ground towards the shelter of the tall cliff.

The rocks were cracked and fissured after the manner of limestone and he managed to find a shallow nook which, though cramped, offered protection from the snow. Here he rested, feeling the strength coming back into his young limbs, and warmth tingling back into his frozen fingers.

He ached desperately and he could feel congealed blood on his lips and from a wound on his forehead but he knew he was not seriously injured, that no bones were broken. What worried him more was the realisation that he could remember nothing of how he came to be there. His mind was like a fog and trying to remember was like groping through the banks of mists. Vague memories appeared and then vanished again before they could be grasped— only one came through with any force: the memory of a blinding lilac flash and an awful sensation of falling, falling . . .

This made him start in fear, to grasp the walls of his little cave as though he might fall out of that too. A sense of panic gripped his throat and he had to stop himself from dashing wildly out into the night.

When his unreasonable fear subsided he tried again to remember what had happened. Where was he? He couldn't remember. How did he get there? His mind was a blank.

He thought and thought, but the more he tried the more hopeless it all seemed. Then, like a blow to the pit of the stomach, he made a sickening discovery. *He could not even remember who he was!*

Feverishly he searched the deep pockets of his greatcoat for some evidence of identity, but all he found were handfuls of mushy snow, a shilling piece, a copious red kerchief and a pocket knife of the sort used by sailors. These told him nothing.

He hastily unbuttoned his coat in order to search his undergarments, but neither his jacket nor his waistcoat revealed anything of interest except for a sticky humbug sweet which he shoved hungrily into his mouth. Exhausted by his efforts he sank back into his shelter and tried to work it all out.

This much was certain: he was lost, cold and hungry.

Furthermore, it seemed unlikely that any help would be forthcoming in the immediate future, for as far as he could judge his situation was one of remoteness, in some barren, hilly country. His other problems could safely wait until later—his immediate need was to reach help, to make contact with civilisation.

The need for action seemed to come instinctively from some ancestral fighting spirit, and he felt the better for it. Wrapping his collar round his ears he pushed himself out of his little cave into the whirling snowflakes. He had no idea which way to go; leaving that to chance he just stumbled wherever his footsteps took him.

It was hard going, over ground which was rough and masked by the soft new snow. Often he stumbled over boulders and potholes, reawakening the pain of his bruises, but he felt that at least he was doing something to help himself, and the activity kept him warm.

He wished that the snow would stop falling. The gently swirling flakes blotted out everything beyond his immediate vicinity so that all sense of time and distance was lost. Once or twice he was sure that he recognized places he had passed before and the thought struck him that he might be walking round in circles, though he had no certain way of knowing and all he could do was to keep walking and hope for the best.

It stopped snowing quite suddenly. One moment all was mist and darkness and the next the clouds rolled back and a bright winter's moon lit a magic landscape.

He found himself standing on a knoll with a deep gorge behind him, showing dark against the snowy hills. Facing him was a wide vale bounded on the one hand by low rolling hills and on the other by a much higher edge. Everything lay clothed in the purest white, and though

there was no sign of habitation it looked a friendly landscape, quite unlike the rocky gorge from which he had
just escaped.

But fine though the view was it was as nothing compared
with the high mountain which seemed to rear almost
immediately overhead. It was a huge mound whose side
had been sheared away as though by a mighty sword-
stroke leaving a great flat face. Snow lay ribboned on it
and in the shifting moonlight first one facet and then
another glittered in a way which made the whole thing
seem vibrant and alive.

There was something about the way the great face
shimmered which stirred his memory; as though he had
heard of such a mountain long, long ago, but he knew it
was useless trying to remember. Nevertheless he felt that
it was a link with his past and he gazed at it with affection,
taking in every detail of its weird, magnificent form.

With the passing of the snowstorm a chill wind had
sprung from the east urging him to be on the move again.
He plunged down through soft snow towards the friendly
vale.

How long he walked he couldn't tell, but it seemed an
eternity. There were stone walls he had to clamber over
and snowdrifts he ploughed through, and he was desperately tired when at last he came to the end of the vale
where it narrowed and turned a sharp corner of hillside
to plunge into a clough or ravine. Here, sheltered by the
enfolding moors, was a small copse and beside it a neat
stone farmhouse, half buried in the drifted snow but with
windows aglow with candlelight.

Summoning his last reserves of energy the boy staggered
down the slopes towards the welcome light. Dogs barked
as he approached but he scarcely heard them. He found

a small postern gate in an ancient wall from which a trodden path led him to the main building. A flagged porch guarded a heavy nailed door and as he beat on wood with his fist the dogs redoubled their barking.

Inside the house he could hear a sound like muffled curses and the clatter of clogs on a stone floor. Bolts scraped back and the door was flung open allowing a flood of light to fall on the boy. A man, thick set and dressed in rough working breeches and shirt, stood ready to receive the late visitor. Behind him, the boy could see two women, hanging back, afraid.

At the sight of the boy with his ragged clothes and face streaked with dirt and blood, the man took a step back in surprise and the women let out a cry of alarm.

The boy staggered forward. 'I, I—,' he croaked. Then his head began to swim, and his legs buckled beneath him. 'My God, Martha!' he heard the man cry. 'This young 'un's half deed!' Then he fainted.

When consciousness returned his first impressions were of comfort and warmth. After the past few hours of terrible ordeal the contrast was so great that he could do nothing except close his eyes again, allowing the sense of safety and well being soak into him. For a while he dozed, but then he had a dream of falling, and he awoke with a start and sat up.

He found himself on a straw bed in front of an enormous open fire, glowing bright with hot coals. The light from the fire was aided by a couple of candles stuck into bottles on a great oak table, but even these failed to light fully the large kitchen which comprised his surroundings.

On the other side of the hearth a young girl of about his own age lay curled on the hard flagged floor fast asleep. The man who had opened the door to him was likewise sleeping seated at the table, his head cradled in his massive brown arms, snoring sonorously. On another chair sat a woman of indeterminate middle age, dressed in drab country clothes, but with a kind face and ready smile.

'Where am I?' The boy asked.

'Nook Hall,' the woman replied in a strong North Country voice, but before he could ask any more questions she silenced him by saying, 'Now hush thi' noise and drink this. Tha' looks fair starved.' From an iron pot on the fire she ladled soup into a bowl and handed it to him. 'Mind now! It's hot,' she warned, as he took the welcome bowl. She went to the table and cut him two thick slices of a dark rye bread.

He ate the bread and soup ravenously. Until that moment he had scarcely realised how hungry he was, but the thick pea soup, flavoured with mutton and strong herbs, sent new life coursing through his veins. Not until he had finished every drop did he lay the bowl down with a contented sigh.

'There's nowt like a bowl o' soup on a cowd neet,' the woman commented, picking up the bowl. 'Though what tha was doing on t'moors at a' beats me. Mester will want a word wi' thi.' She went over to the slumbering man and shook him roughly. 'Sam! Sam!' she bellowed in his ear. 'Young 'un's waked up!'

Sam did not feel at all inclined to follow the boy's example and it was only after considerable shaking that he at last raised his head and rubbed the sleep from his eyes with much grunting and a few muttered curses, by which time the young girl was awake also, disturbed by the commotion.

Sam was a big man—well over six feet tall and broad in proportion. His hair was thick and black, his face strong and tanned like old leather by a life of outdoor toil. Yet despite his size he was not a frightening man; there was about him an air of tolerance such as big men often have. He came over to the boy and gazed down at him, speculatively.

'Well, young 'un. Tha looks a seet better than when I last saw thee,' he said, grinning. This was true indeed; in the couple of hours that had passed since he fainted at the door these homely folk had washed his face and hands, bandaged his wounded head, and removed his outer garments for much needed repairs.

'I thank you, sir, for your hospitality,' the boy replied with formal courtesy. 'May I ask to whom I am indebted?'

'Tha speaks wi' a fair tongue, lad, an' that's for sure,' Sam replied. 'Educated, I'll warrant! My name's Sam Ollershaw, an' this is Martha, my wife, and dowter Betsy. We farms Nook Hall for our sins, like all t'Ollershaws this last three hunderd year or more—God knows how we've stuck it that long,' he added philosophically.

'You have saved my life, sir, and I am deeply grateful.'

'Happen we did at that,' Sam replied frankly. 'But how come tha was wanderin' on t'moors on a dark winter's neet?'

Martha Ollershaw and Betsy drew nearer to the fire to listen to the boy unfold his strange tale. He told them how he had found himself lying in the snow, wounded, how he was lost, and how he at last found Nook Hall. As the various incidents were related the women clucked sympathetically. Sam remained silent.

' 'Tis a strange tale tha tells, reet enough,' he said when the boy finished. 'And tha cannot remember thi name?'

'I remember nothing, sir, before that dreadful journey through the snow to your door.' He didn't mention the lilac flash and the sense of falling; they seemed of no account, hallucinations brought on by his injuries.

'Well, I've heerd on such things afore,' Sam conceded, 'but on t'other hand tha might be a 'prentice lad run away fro' thi mester.' At this the boy looked blank; it was plain he hadn't the faintest idea what Sam was talking about.

'Use thi sense, Sam Ollershaw,' said Martha from the hearthside settle, where she had resumed the repair of the boy's torn greatcoat. 'Whoever seed a Charity lad wi' clothes like these? Come to that, whoever seed a Charity lad wi' ony clothes worth callin'?'

Sam allowed that there was good sense in his wife's reasoning and that it was unlikely the boy was an apprentice.

'Excuse me, sir,' the boy remarked puzzled, 'but what is a 'prentice?'

'A 'prentice? Why, he's a lad serving his time to a trade, so as he might learn it and become a journeyman or craftsman. Theer's nowt as comes natural to ony mon—it's getten to be learnt, and so a 'prentice learns from his mester.'

'Why then!' the boy exclaimed. 'If I was a 'prentice learning my trade I should hardly be running away, surely?'

Sam laughed. 'Aye, lad, so tha might think—only some mesters are fair hard on t'lads, see. Especially in some o' t'cotton mills.'

Martha, who had been engrossed in her stitching, let out a sudden cry of surprise. 'Now theer's a funny thing,' she said. 'This coats getten a label—wi' a name on it!' She held it up for them to see.

'Here, Betsy!' ordered Sam to his daughter. 'Tha's been to t'parson's day school—what does it say?'

The girl took the coat and held the label to the firelight that she might read it better. Her learning was slight, but she struggled bravely with the unfamiliar letters.

'It says *Josiah Small, Tailor, Spanish Town*.'

'Spanish Town?' Sam echoed. 'Why that's in the Indies!'

'Happen that's why he's so brown and handsome,' said Betsy shyly. 'They do say as the sun shines in t'Indies all the time.'

'Aye, but it don't tell us how he came to be on t'moor,' her father commented. He appealed to the boy, 'Cawn't thee remember owt, lad? The Indies?'

The boy shook his head sadly.

Sam paced up and down the room, thinking hard. 'Yon coat was made for thee and no other,' he reasoned aloud. 'That means tha must have been in t'Indies. And tha skin is so brown that tha must have been theer noan so long ago. Theer's only one explanation—tha's coom off a ship i' Liverpool: one o' them Indies slavin' ships as Mr. Wilberforce is allus rantin' about. Though how tha geet to Derbyshire—'

But his wife interrupted his monologue. 'Well, happen that can keep till t'morn,' she said firmly. 'T'lad's fair wore out an' so are we.' Without waiting for any reply she pushed the boy gently but firmly back into the straw bed and laid a thick wool blanket over him. He was so tired that he fell instantly asleep.

Martha ushered Sam and Betsy from the room, off to bed. Before she too departed she took one of the candles from the table and held it over the sleeping boy, so as to get a better look at his face. Poor child! She thought: no home, no name—probably a runaway midshipman if truth be known—and such a handsome boy. As the candlelight flickered over his unconscious features, Martha noticed for the first time that he wore round his neck a thin silver chain. Instinctively curious she bent down and gently undid the clasp by which the chain was fastened then lifted it into the light. On the end of the chain was a small silver medallion engraved with three heraldic stars.

The pendant gave Martha an idea—just a vague, half-formed notion. She tucked it into her dress and crept quietly to bed.

CHAPTER TWO

CHAPEL EN LE FRITH

AN ITINERANT PEDLAR, on his way from Castleton to Chapel en le Frith, brought news of the tragedy in the Winnats Pass to Nook Hall next day.

He was an engaging rogue, well versed in the art of story telling, which he used as an incentive for people to buy his wares, and he spared Martha Ollershaw none of the tragic details. It seemed that a lead miner, on the way to his work on Eldon Hill had come across the smashed coach near the foot of Winnats Pass. Further investigation had resulted in the discovery of two horribly battered corpses, a man and a woman, both elderly. Who they were or whence they came was a mystery, no luggage or papers had been found, which was not surprising considering the terrible force of the accident.

The story had an even greater effect on his listener than the pedlar had hoped. Martha went white, and thanking the pedlar for his tale, hurriedly purchased a reel of thread and without waiting for the small change dashed indoors. The man stared after her in amazement, then, with a shrug, he pocketed the coins and continued on his journey.

When Martha recounted the pedlar's tale to her husband he nodded in silent understanding. 'It explains everythin',' he said when she had finished. 'T'young 'un were in t'coach along o' his parents. Then summat happened—like as not t'horses bowted—an' he were thrown clear.'

'No wonder he lost his senses, poor lad,' said Martha. 'Aye, a knock on t'head can do strange things to a chap,' said Sam. 'Like as not, his memory's gone for good.'

His wife gave him a shrewd sideways glance. 'What's to become of him?' she asked.

'Tha knows as weel as I do,' Sam replied. 'He were fount i' this parish and t'parish mon look after him, by law. Ony orphan becomes a charge on t'parish rates.'

Martha sighed. It was quite true what Sam had said, that the boy was now legally the responsibility of the Parish Officers of Chapel en le Frith. She had hoped that he would have said more—that he would have wanted to keep the boy at the farm, to be brought up as their own son. After all, Sam had always wanted a son; somebody he could take pride in and to whom he could leave Nook Hall. The boy was such a fine lad too, handsome and strong.

As if he could read his wife's thoughts, Sam said, 'He's a fine lad, Martha—but he's noan a babe ony moor. He's fourteen if he's a day; comin' on to manhood, and a mon must mak his own decisions.'

He put a strong brown arm round his wife's shoulders and gave her a tender look. 'I know what tha' thinkin', lass,' he said softly. 'But first we mun tell t'young 'un how he stands.'

They found the boy in the stables, helping Betsy to feed the horses with hay from a loft. A night's rest seemed to have revived all the energy of his young frame, and though his head was still bandaged, it did nothing to stop him laughing and joking with Betsy. When Sam and his wife made their appearance, Betsy ran over and cried, laughingly, 'Fayther, fayther! Do stop un from teasin' me so!'

'Aw reet lass, aw reet!' said her father, calming her boisterous spirits. 'Ah've geet summat t'say to t'young 'un.' There was such a serious look on his face that the girl's smile died on her lips. The boy sprang down from the loft, anxious to hear the news.

Sam told the story plainly, without any of the pedlar's melodrama, and as he spoke he watched the boy's face. He saw it register sadness, but there were no tears, and when he had finished the boy thanked him gravely. 'It makes me sad that my parents should perish in such a fashion,' he said in a low voice, 'but I cannot weep for them—I cannot even remember what they looked like. Of the coach journey or the accident, I have no recollection. It seems to me that I was born yesterday!'

Betsy flung her arms about him to comfort him. He smiled at her, then looking at Sam asked, 'What is to become of me?'

'Well, by reets, tha becomes a ward o' t'Parish Officers,' said Sam.

'And what will they do?' demanded the boy.

'Bind thee 'prentice to a master till tha twenty-one. That road tha costs 'em nowt and tha learns a trade.'

'What sort of trade, sir?'

Sam frowned. 'Well, tha't a bit too big to mak a chimney sweep—like as not tha'd be sent to a cotton mill.'

'No!' Betsy cried aloud. 'Tha cawn't send him to a mill, fayther. 'Taint human! Why cawn't he stay at Nook Hall wi' us?' And she began to weep.

The boy looked embarrassed. ' 'Twould not be right to impose on your father and mother any more, Betsy,' he said consolingly. 'You have all been so kind as it is.'

'Stuff!' cried Martha Ollershaw. 'Tha con stay as long as tha wants, lad!'

'Well, I don't know . . .'

Martha looked at her husband as though he exasperated her. 'For God's sake say summat, Sam Ollershaw,' she cried. 'Tell the lad he's reet welcome to stay.'

Sam cleared his throat and tried to look stern, but failed signally to achieve anything but a grin. 'If tha wants to stop on at Nook Hall lad, then us'll be reet glad to hev thee,' he said.

Betsy let out a whoop of delight and Martha threw her arms around her husband and hugged him. Sam shook the boy's hand. 'Tha will be wantin' a name,' he said.

'We'll call him Jeremy Ollershaw,' Martha said firmly.

Sam looked at his wife and smiled. He knew why she had chosen that name. Fifteen years ago they had buried their infant son, and he too had been Jeremy. Had he survived the colic, he might well have looked like this strong youngster who had so dramatically entered into their lives.

Jeremy quickly settled into his new life and the tragedy of the Winnats Pass, even the mystery of his own origins receded into the background of his thoughts. A bedroom had been found for him under the flagged roof of the ancient farmhouse, and though at first it looked a dusty, dreary cubicle through not having been used for half a century, it soon brightened under the hard scrubbing and polishing of Betsy, who made it her special care. Clothes, too, were found: a rough cotton shirt and coarse knee-breeches held up by a broad buckled leather belt, for the fact of the matter was that although Jeremy's own clothes were of fine worsted they would never have survived daily use on a rough moorland farm. So his suit was carefully folded away for Sunday best, and his shoes, too, fine leather with real silver buckles, were replaced by a hard but serviceable footwear which Sam called *clogs*. These clogs had wooden soles which clattered with a fine noise on the flagged floors of Nook Hall, and though at first they hurt Jeremy's feet, he was very proud of them.

For the first week or so Jeremy had to be content with looking at the world through the little diamond panes on the farm windows. Mrs. Ollershaw had very definite ideas on how a sick boy should be treated, and until his head wound was completely healed Jeremy was not to be allowed outdoors. He was fed with mutton broth and gruel and sent early to bed : food, sleep and no hard work were the cornerstones of Martha Ollershaw's remedy.

It certainly made Jeremy strong and healthy, though he was impatient to be out helping Sam on the farm. The snow, he observed through the windows, was gradually thawing, and one day he looked out and found it gone completely.

He had plenty of time for exploring the old farmhouse. Nook Hall was larger than it seemed. The kitchen, where the family spent most of their time indoors, was quite enormous, almost like a small barn. It was hung with a miscellany of pots and pans in iron and copper and even two or three pairs of the evil looking shears used for cutting the wool off sheep. Huge hams, salted and smoked, hung from dark beams, and it seemed to Jeremy that whatever else happened at Nook Hall the occupants would never starve !

Dark, cavernous passages connected with other rooms downstairs, one of which, at the front of the house, was finely proportioned and lined with wainscoting. The ceiling was finished in a plaster relief of flowers and sea shells which made Jeremy gasp in awe, for he thought it extremely beautiful. When he asked Martha about it she told him that it was the 'best' room, reserved for very important occasions like weddings and funerals.

The stairs to the bedrooms were narrow and steep and the rooms themselves had nothing of the proportions of those downstairs. For the most part they were small, with wattled partitions and low ceilings, lit by tiny casements through which the light filtered in a strange greenish hue caused by the ancient glass. Nobody could have described Nook Hall as luxurious, though it had a certain spartan comfort which reflected the austerity of the landscape in which it stood.

Martha and Betsy between them kept the house as clean and tidy as one might expect, and yet, as Jeremy wandered round he had a sad feeling that the Hall had known better days. He asked Sam about bygone times, and by way of reply the farmer led him to the front door over which was carved a date.

'That's when her was built,' he said proudly. '1550, and her's been standin' here ever sin—two hunnerd and forty-five year. An' ah'll tell thee summat else, Jeremy lad; theer's bin an Ollershaw here aw that time.'

'It's a big house, sir,' said Jeremy.

Sam sighed and said, 'Aye—a seet *too* big for these hard times. It were aw reet long ago when these moors were as thick wi' sheep as buttercups in a meadow, an' good English wool were on every mon's back, but not now. It's cotton now lad; cotton as can be spun and weaved i' great mills usin' the new machinery of Mr. Hargreaves and Mr. Arkwright. Mak no mistake, lad, cotton is king now!'

With the return of milder weather and the improvement to Jeremy's wound, Martha Ollershaw finally relented and allowed the boy outdoors to help Sam around the farm.

Not that there was a great deal he could do. Nook Hall had an extensive acreage of moorland, but it was almost exclusively devoted to sheep; miserable scraggy animals kept in bounds by long dry-stone walls. In fact, it was the repair of these walls which occupied most of the short winter days and Jeremy was fascinated at the way in which Sam could fit together the bits and pieces of grit-stone into a solid wall without so much as a dab of mortar.

'It's just a knack wi't'stones,' said Sam modestly, when Jeremy asked how it was done. 'Tha mun hev an ee for t'reet bit.' And he picked up a flat stone from the field. 'This is a bonny bit as should goo reet theer,' and he pushed the stone into place at the end of a newly con-structed length of wall. 'See how it lies? It kegs innart—towards t'centre o' t'wall.' He placed another piece on the other side, and that too leaned inwards so that the two bits pressed against one another. 'Now sithee, they cawn't faw out, 'cos Nature maks un press together. One balances t'other.'

'Yes I see now,' said Jeremy. 'And the longer they remain the more they will settle, becoming ever firmer.'

'That's reet. Then to tie it aw together we caps t'wall wi' a layer o' stones lyin' cross-wise.'

It sounded so simple that Jeremy asked whether he might try it, and Sam readily agreed, though not without a grin.

Jeremy met with little success. Somehow, no matter how carefully he tried, the stones would not lock together as they did for Sam and he grew increasingly impatient. At last, when fifteen minutes' work suddenly collapsed in a heap of rubble he cried angrily, 'A plague on these stones!'

Sam let out a great laugh. 'Now, now, lad! Howd thi' temper,' he remonstrated mildly. 'Tha' cawn't expect to learn it aw in a day. I towd thi—it taks an ee for stones, and that don't come easy.'

On the next morning, which was bright and sparkling with winter sunshine, Sam announced that they would climb to the top of the big hill which dominated Nook Hall and where there was a boundary wall he wanted to inspect. Jeremy was pleased at this news, for from the summit of the hill he expected to see the surrounding countryside of which he was totally ignorant.

The climb made his legs ache, though Sam seemed to stroll up the steep grass slopes without effort, and he was glad when at last they reached the top.

A scene of incomparable inhospitality met Jeremy's amazed eyes. Instead of a true summit he discovered that he had reached a mere knoll on a vast barren plateau which seemed to stretch away to the horizon. The grass was coarse and brown, glinting here and there with frozen bog-water. Patches of cotton grass, with white tufts looking like a thousand rabbits' tails, showed how sour the land was and there were even places where nothing grew at all; sombre peat bogs eroded with deeply cut dykes, or *groughs*. In one or two instances weird gritstone rocks, black and rounded, rose from the moor in frenetic pinnacles which looked like the work of the Devil.

Jeremy shuddered, and Sam, quick to note his reaction, said 'Aye, it's nowt to write whoam about, is it? Yon's cawd High Peak Forest, and o'er theer, beyond them black tors, tha con see Kyndwr Scwd, which ah've heerd tell on as t'highest mountain i' the Realm.'

'It's a wild place right enough,' agreed Jeremy. 'I should hate to lose myself there.' And he thought of his recent flight and how differently things might have turned out had he been misfortunate enough to wander into the High Peak.

Sam then drew his attention the other way, looking down on Nook Hall which seemed like a toy farm, so far above it were they, and beyond the farm to the lower and greener hills of the south.

'What a contrast!' Jeremy exclaimed.

'Yon's limestone country,' Sam explained. 'No bogs theer, but caves wheer men dig for lead an' short green grass which is good for t'sheep.'

'And trees too.'

'Trees and aw. Tha gets no trees on these moors, but yon country is full on 'em. 'Tis a pretty country, yon.'

'It does not seem possible that two such different lands could exist side by side,' said Jeremy, full of wonder.

' 'Tis strange, reet enough, but 'tis not for simple folk like us to question God's will. Tha con see as clear as crystal wheer one ends and t'other begins.'

It was true enough what Sam said. The dark gritstone areas stood out in sharp contrast with the softer green of the limestone land. It was almost as if there was an irregular but quite definite boundary between the two, forming totally different worlds.

'What's yonder village?' enquired Jeremy, pointing to some distant wisps of smoke curling into the clear sky.

'Why that's Chapel en le Frith, lad. Tha'll see enough o' that afore long!'

In fact, the Ollershaw's visited Chapel en le Frith every market day. Sometimes Sam went alone, but usually they went as a family with Martha and Betsy selling whatever produce they had to offer. So it was that the following week Jeremy went with them.

His first impression of the village was not very favourable. A straggle of grey cottages ran along the highway, mounting steeply up an incline, or brow as Sam called it, until at the top they met a small market square. Some larger houses and an inn enclosed this precinct and behind these again there were more cottages and a church. Everything was built of the sombre coloured gritstone and as the day itself was grey the overall effect was melancholy.

Though the village itself was drab it was enlivened on that market day by the numbers of people who were coming in from the farms and hamlets round about. Some were on foot, carrying baskets of produce for sale (Martha and Betsy had a large basket of eggs), others came in on mud-spattered carts which creaked and jolted in the ruts of the highway. Some of the women were dressed in their Sunday apparel as though they intended to combine business with a social occasion such as a visit to a friend, but most wore their plain working dresses with aprons called *pinnies*, and a long woven head shawl. Almost without exception they wore clogs, the clatter of which added to the general din of the market day.

In the square itself stalls were set out with produce of every description, including cottons from the local mills and silks from the Indies. Between the stalls other vendors were selling their wares from baskets on the flagged pavement and several pedlars strolled around crying their goods to anyone who wanted to listen.

At one side of the square some children were having a merry game tormenting a poor fellow who lay stretched out on the ground with his feet firmly clasped in the stocks. Jeremy thought he must be some desperate criminal to be so harshly treated but when he mentioned it to Sam the latter just laughed and said it was 'nobbut owd

Jem Clough who allus got drunk on a market day afore noon and was locked up as a lesson in sobriety'.

Martha and Betsy set their basket down in a free space and began selling the eggs they had brought. Sam announced that he had some business to attend to and promised that he would be as quick as he could.

'Tha's no hurry,' his wife said. 'When we've sowd t'eggs ah've getten a bit o' business o' mi own to see to.'

Sam's face broke into a broad grin, and winking slyly at Jeremy, as though sharing a joke he said, 'Tha noan goo-in for t'see yon owd faggot Becca again?'

Martha bridled and replied sharply, 'Thee mind thi own business, Sam Ollershaw, an' ah'll mind mine! Theer's some folk as would come a long way for t'see Becca.'

'Aye—them as has moor money than sense!' Her husband retorted. But he wasn't angry, Jeremy noted, he was just chaffing her.

'Who is Owd Becca?' Jeremy asked as they strolled together across the square, leaving the women to their business.

'Owd Becca? Why, her's t'famous Witch o' Chapel,' said Sam, not without a little pride in his voice. 'Theer's them as reckons her con see into a mon's future, or cure a sickness, aye, or put a curse on an enemy! Mesel', ah reckon her's nobbut a harmless owd besom, takin' shillin's off gormless country wenches like our Martha. But 'tis true folk come aw t'way from London to see her sometimes.'

'I suppose if she were really bad, she would be locked up in the stocks like poor Mr Clough,' said Jeremy.

'Ah'd like for t'see the mon as would try!' said Sam with a laugh. 'Owd Becca might be a fraud but her's noan a fool as well. Wi' aw the brass her's made her's bowt up hafe o' Chapel—there's a good few folk puttin' on airs i' this town who owe their roof to Owd Becca, I con tell thi.'

They had reached the front of an inn called the *Kings Head*; a large building by local standards, occupying one corner of the market square. Here Sam left Jeremy, giving him fourpence to spend on victuals if he should feel hungry and telling him that he would not be long away.

Jeremy pocketed the coins and peered curiously into the doorway of the inn. The place was doing a lively trade as might be expected on market day and the interior was noisy, dark and smoky, so that Jeremy was afraid to go inside. He resolved to wait awhile until hunger forced him into such a noisy place; meanwhile there was plenty to watch in the street.

He had been standing around for five or ten minutes when there was a sudden bustle at the top end of the street and a fine coach and pair came creaking round a bend, its driver struggling against the potholes of the road and cursing the pedestrians who got in his way. 'Make way!' he bawled. 'Make way on the King's Highway!' And the people fell back though one or two of the farm lads hurled good natured epithets at the driver.

The coach rolled to a halt by the inn door and the driver, seeing Jeremy standing idly by called out to him, 'You there, boy! Hand down this trunk and there's a penny for you!' From behind his driving seat the man pulled a small leather portmanteau.

Jeremy stepped forward briskly. He did not in the least mind helping these newcomers, whoever they were, and the prospect of another penny pleased him. Added to those Sam had already given him he would be passing rich!

He grasped the edge of the trunk and tugged it until it slid off the coach roof into his arms. He was surprised by its unexpected weight. His knees buckled slightly, but he managed to turn round and stagger towards the door of the inn.

At the very instant that Jeremy reached the doorway a tall young man came swaggering out. Jeremy cried out a warning, but too late. They cannoned into each other, and Jeremy, off balance, let the trunk fall. It landed heavily on the other's foot.

The young man gave a cry mingled with rage and pain as though he did not know which was hurt the most, his foot or his dignity. Then it seemed, he caught sight of Jeremy's countenance for the first time and a look of sheer surprise came over his face, to be quickly replaced by pure malice.

'You clumsy young fool!' he shouted. 'I'll teach you to go barging into people!'

He was a well built fellow, quite six foot in height, and perhaps nineteen years of age. He was obviously not a working man for his suit was of fine blue broadcloth, trimmed with lace at the collar and pockets, and he wore silver silk hose and patent leather shoes. In his hand he carried an ebony cane surmounted by a silver knob.

With a vicious swipe he struck Jeremy across the side of the head, sending him sprawling on the pavement.

'Get up, you young swine, and take what's coming to you!' he cried, and he raised the cane again as if to strike Jeremy where he lay.

But the cane never descended. A strong hand grasped it from behind and wrenched it from the bully's grasp.

An excited crowd had gathered at the outset of the incident and now it gave a gasp of expectation at this new turn to the affair. Everyone stared at the man who had grasped the cane. He had stepped from the coach. Not very tall, but extraordinarily broad for his height, he appeared to be about thirty years old, and his face, rugged and sun-tanned, bore the unmistakable marks of the Jewish race. He was dressed in the height of London fashion: a pale blue striped waistcoat under his jacket and canary yellow silk hose which made him look something of the dandy. A lace kerchief protruded from one cuff.

'Let the boy be,' he said in a strong London accent, heavily overlaid with genteel refinement. 'Why, stap me fellow! 'Twas a pure accident.'

Jeremy's assailant went white with rage. 'Why, you damned dandy!' He roared. 'Give me my cane back! I'll teach thee to interfere with Harrison Bradwell!'

He lunged at the Jew with a blow which would have stunned an ox had it connected, but the latter simply stepped nimbly to one side and Bradwell went sprawling into the arms of the crowd.

'A feight! A feight!' The crowd shouted in bloodthirsty delight.

' 'Pon my soul, sir,' the Jew mocked. 'What a demmed impetuous fellow you are, to be sure.'

Bradwell snarled an incoherent reply and rushed once again to the attack. The Jew easily avoided him, then, much to the amusement of the crowd, adopted a strange posture with his left arm half extended before him and his right held close to his chest, both fists closed. He looked so comical that some of the crowd laughed and all were quite certain that the burly Bradwell would flatten him.

But the laughter soon died when the Jew, always dancing out of Bradwell's reach, began to hammer away with his left fist at Bradwell's head. Like a rapier the fist darted in and out. Tap! Tap! Tap! And Bradwell could do nothing to stop it. All he could do was to make mad bull-like rushes which his nimble adversary easily avoided, and all the time that wicked left fist tapped away.

Within minutes Bradwell's face was a gory mess, blood streaming from his busted nose on to his fine clothes. He was visibly weaker, too, and his wild swings began to assume the characteristics of a man facing desperate humiliation. Then, as if he was suddenly tired of the whole affair, the Jew whipped his right hand across Bradwell's chin so fast that most of those watching missed it, and Bradwell slumped unconscious to the ground as though he had been pole-axed.

A great cheer went up from the crowd, and if it was mostly appreciation at the dramatic way the fight had finished, it was also quite obvious that Harrison Bradwell was not over popular and they were cheering his downfall.

The Jew smiled wryly at the jubilation, and seeking out Jeremy said, 'Come, boy, let us repair inside for refreshment.' People slapped them both good-naturedly on their backs by way of congratulation and just as they were about to step inside, a soldier, dressed in the uniform of one of the Foot Regiments, sprang forward and grasped the Jew's hand. 'Well done, Mr Mendoza, sir!' he cried enthusiastically. 'I saw 'ee fight at Blackheath last summer when 'ee beat the Dutchman. Reckon Bradwell didn't know he was up agin the great Daniel Mendoza!'

At the mention of Mendoza's name another great shout of appreciation went up from the crowd. There was not a man present that had not heard of the legendary Daniel Mendoza; the champion prizefighter of the world!

Inside the inn the landlord hurried to find them a

comfortable alcove next to the blazing coal fire and almost as soon as they were seated a serving wench came and laid on the little table mugs of ale, a plate of cold beef and a huge ham pie.

Mendoza took a pull of ale from his tankard and indicated to Jeremy that he should help himself to the food.

'What do they call you, boy?' he asked, delicately drying his lips with his lace kerchief.

'Jeremy, sir,' the youngster replied.

'Well, Jeremy, you came as near to being killed by that scoundrel Bradwell as e'er I saw. Had I not interfered he would have done thee for sure—what ails the fellow? Is there a feud between your families?'

'No, sir. I never saw him before today. I think he was just angered that I dropped the trunk on his foot.'

' 'Strordinary,' mused Mendoza. 'I was watching the incident and it seemed to me that the blackguard's face was a positive mask of *hatred*. Anger I could understand, but hatred . . . 'strordinary!' And he bit off a large portion of ham pie.

'I have yet to thank you, sir, for coming to my rescue,' said Jeremy shyly.

'Demmed civil of thee, boy. Shows good breedin',' said Mendoza, his mouth full of pie. 'But 'twere nothing. The man is an untutored boor. A country clod, unversed in the manly art of self defence, and not the sort of fellow I would normally soil my mitts on. Mind thee; I needed the exercise after that demmed drive from Manchester.'

'He was a big fellow, sir, yet you are unmarked; indeed scarcely winded. You must be a very good fighter,' said Jeremy.

Mendoza laughed pleasantly. 'By m'faith, 'tis true enough, though it's never been said to my face before,' he chortled. 'Fighting—prizefighting—has been my living, young sir, and you must be one of the few boys in England who has not heard of Daniel Mendoza! As a matter of fact—just between ourselves, you understand—I practically invented the game. I gave it form and grace. Did ye notice, for instance, how I stood square on to the ruffian and kept poking my left fist in his face? My own invention, sir, my own invention—I call it keeping a straight left. Come I'll show you.'

Mendoza jumped up full of enthusiasm and faced the somewhat less enthusiastic Jeremy. 'Don't be afraid, I'll not hurt ye,' he said encouragingly.

Jeremy adopted the peculiar stance which Mendoza employed, and the latter thrust forward his chin as a target. 'Hit that!' He commanded.

Jeremy poked out his clenched right fist, but scarcely had it travelled more than a few inches when it was powerfully blocked. As he withdrew his arm to try again, Mendoza tapped him smartly on the nose, bringing water to the boy's eyes. Jeremy dropped his hands in surprise—in consequence of which he received two more smart taps.

'Keep your mitts up, boy!' commanded the prizefighter.

Within a few minutes Jeremy began to grow accustomed to the peculiar stance and the constant jigging motion of the fight game. He found that he could keep his balance and block punches, and once or twice he managed to catch Mendoza with a light blow, though the prizefighter didn't seem to mind this at all. At last, after ten minutes' exercise, Mendoza cried a halt.

'Enough!' he said with a grin, sitting down again at the table. ' 'Tis hot work fighting in a tavern!' He took a long pull at his ale mug. 'Well, Jeremy lad, at least you know how to defend yourself now. Remember always *box clever*—indeed some of the bucks who come to my gymnasium in London have taken to calling it boxing. And now—what about another slice of this most excellent ham pie?'

When Jeremy had eaten his fill he bade good-bye to Mr Mendoza, and thanked him for all he had done. He hurried out of the inn, afraid that he might have missed Sam in all the excitement, but he need not have worried for as he emerged into the market square he caught sight of the farmer coming down the main street.

Sam had been visiting a friend at the far side of Chapel as a consequence of which he knew nothing of Jeremy's adventures. He listened to the boy's tale with a face which registered both surprise and consternation.

'Ah'm reet glad as Harrison Bradwell geet a hidin','' he said, when Jeremy finished his story. 'But tha con bank on one thing—he'll noan forget it. Tha'll hev to watch out for yon mon, Jeremy—he's a nasty bit o'work, an' no mistake!'

They strolled down the hill towards the cross-roads.

'We are not waiting for Martha and Betsy then?' enquired Jeremy.

'Nay, lad. Happen they'll be hours yet. When t'wommen-folk get jawing wi' Owd Becca, there's no knowin' what time they'll finish! Ah wonders sometimes what they finds for t'talk abaht!'

In fact, Martha Ollershaw had just given the Witch of Chapel a little silver pendant, engraved with three stars; the very one she had taken from Jeremy's neck on the night of his arrival at Nook Hall. And though none of them knew it at the time, it was to save Jeremy's life.

2*

CHAPTER THREE

BOUND APPRENTICE

EARLY ON THE third day after their visit to Chapel en le Frith, Sam and Jeremy were at work repairing the roof of the byre when they heard the clop of a horse's hooves on the farm lane. At once they looked up to see who the visitor might be, for Nook Hall was well off the route of most travellers, and they saw a rather elderly man frail of body and with a sallow countenance which spoke of the clerk's trade, approaching. He was dressed all in grey, in clothes which were out of fashion and thread-bare.

The rider doffed his broad-brimmed hat when he saw them, and approaching the gate called out, 'Be this Nook Hall?'

'Aye,' replied Sam, with typical north-country caution.

'Then do I have the pleasure of addressing Mister Samuel Ollershaw?' His voice had only the faintest trace of dialect.

'That's ma name,' affirmed Sam. 'What's tha business?'

'Mister Jebediah Crew, at your service, sir—Clerk to the Justices at Chapel in the County of Derby.' He spoke his title with obvious pride, but if he expected Sam Ollershaw to be overcome with awe he was quickly disappointed. Seeing that Sam made no comment the clerk continued, 'I am instructed to speak with you, sir, on a matter of some import.'

'Concerning what?' asked Sam, curious.

'Concerning yonder boy, unless I'm much mistaken,' replied the other.

A strange inexplicable fear gripped Sam's throat, and he saw Jeremy throw him a questioning glance.

'Tha'd best goo inside,' he called down. 'Ah'll join thi presently.'

When Sam and Jeremy entered the kitchen they found the clerk warming his hands by the customary huge fire.

' 'Tis a raw day for riding,' he muttered as they joined him. His thin body looked starved and pinched.

They had the room to themselves. Martha and Betsy had gone over to Chapel Milton to visit a friend who had just had a new baby and they would not be back until late afternoon. Sam wished now that they hadn't gone; there was something about this little clerk which filled him with foreboding and he would have felt stronger for his wife's support.

'Well then, Mester Clerk, what's aw this abaht?' he demanded, mustering as stern a tone as he could.

'It has been brought to the attention of the Justices that you have taken custody of an orphan boy—to wit, this young man standing here.'

'Aye, that's reet enough,' Sam admitted cautiously.

'Doubtless you are aware, sir, that orphans are the responsibility of the Parish Officers?'

'Happen so,' replied Sam. 'But when Jeremy came to us door one dark winter's neet, in need o' care and shelter there wer'nt no Parish Officers around. We took him in, and looked after him, an' now he's one o't'family.'

'Ah! On that we must disagree, Mr Ollershaw,' said the clerk, shrewdly picking up Sam's last remark. 'That you acted with great charity and in a truly Christian spirit, nobody can deny—but the fact remains, the boy is still an orphan.'

Jeremy gave a cry of anger. 'I came to Nook Hall of my own free will,' he cried. 'This is now my home!'

The officer looked at the boy disapprovingly, saying, 'Hold your tongue, sirrah! You have no say in the matter at all. You are a minor—under twenty-one—and as such have no legal rights. Your Fate must be left to the wiser councils of your elders!' Turning to Sam he said, 'You understand, sir, that having failed to make application for legal custody of the child, you have no claim on him?'

'I understand this, mester,' said Sam angrily. 'That we took Jeremy as us own son, an' we're noan gooin' to part wi' him. Aw this argy bargy abaht t'law maks me fair sick—it's fust time as I ever heered on t'Parish wantin' their orphans; they're usually glad to be shut on 'em! However, if it's got to be legal then ah'll ride o'er an' see t'officers misel', this very day!'

The little clerk shook his head. 'Alas! You are too late, Mr Ollershaw,' he said. 'Acting in their official capacity as the boy's rightful guardians, the Parish Officers have indentured him to Mr Joshua Bradwell of Cressdale Mill.'

For a moment there was absolute silence in the great kitchen, both Jeremy and Sam being stunned by the shock of this news. Then, with a violence which the boy had never seen before, Sam sprang at the clerk, eyes blazing and face red with anger. He lifted the little man clean off the floor by his lapels and shook him as though he were no more than a rag doll.

'You lie, damn you!' he roared. ''Tis some trick to tak t'lad away! Ah'll thresh thee within a hafe o'thi life!'

'Put me down, sir, I beg you! Please put me down!'

squealed the terrified clerk. ' 'Tis no doing of mine! I am merely an officer of the court!'

Sam dumped the little man down on a settle. He at once delved into an inner pocket of his coat and drew forth a foolscap parchment which he offered tremblingly to the angry farmer.

Sam glanced over the document. His anger cooled and was replaced by a look of absolute dejection. 'Ah'm noan a hand for readin',' he said despondently. 'But ah recognize t'Justices' signatures, reet enough. These mun be his indentures?'

The clerk nodded silently.

'I'll not go, Sam,' cried Jeremy stoutly. 'I'll be apprentice to no one—and especially not to a Bradwell!'

The clerk, fearing for his life, dared say nothing, but Sam's temper had cooled and his usual good sense asserted itself again. 'Theer's nowt we can do, Jeremy,' he said sadly. 'This is a proper legal document, lad, aw signed an' sealed by t'Justices.'

Seizing his opportunity the clerk added, 'And consider what would happen to Mr Ollershaw if he kept you here. He would be breaking the law, and that would mean prison—possibly transportation to the Australian colonies. What would then become of his family and his farm?'

Jeremy felt as though there were invisible hands clutching at him, dragging him down into a misery neither he nor Sam could fight. He wanted to hit out blindly at his enemies—but what good would it do? And who were his enemies? Some instinct told him that he was in a prepared trap, that this apprenticeship was no mere accident of the law but had been carefully arranged. It was more than a coincidence that the name of Bradwell should appear again and Jeremy knew in his heart that Harrison

Bradwell was behind this. He remembered the fury that Harrison had showed him in Chapel, and he wondered what it was that made the Bradwells so vindictive against an unknown boy. There was nothing he could do but nod acceptance of his fate.

'The terms of your apprenticeship are set out in this document,' the clerk said, feeling more confident now that tempers had cooled. 'The main provisions are as follows:

'That you be bound apprentice to Mr Joshua Bradwell at Cressdale Mill, and that you obey him and serve him loyally until your twenty-first birthday.

'That in return for such loyal service Mr Bradwell will undertake to feed and clothe you and instruct you in the craft of cotton spinning . . . and in addition to which he will ensure that you have a proper Christian upbringing, and instruction in the Gospels, the Catechism, reading and writing.'

The clerk folded the document away into his pocket. 'And now,' he said, 'you will make ready to ride with me. I am instructed to deliver you to the Apprentice House before evening, so 'tis best we leave as soon as possible.'

'I am ready,' the boy replied in a low voice. To Sam he said, 'Thank you for all your kindness, Sam. Remember me to Betsy and Martha—I wish they were here so that I could see them once more before I leave.'

' 'Tis as well ah'm thinkin', or they'd be skrikin' for sure,' said Sam grimly. 'This is tha home, Jeremy, and don't thee forget it. Be it seven year or seventeen, this is wheer tha mun return.'

Ten minutes later Jeremy was mounted on the horse behind the little clerk and they rode away from Nook Hall. The boy cast a backward glance over his shoulder for a last sight of the farm before it disappeared in a fold of the moor, and he wondered whether he would ever see it again.

The doubly laden horse made hard work of the long pull up over the moors from Nook Hall to Sparrowpit. The ancient cross-roads with its famous inn held no appeal for Jeremy, low spirited as he was, but he could not help noticing that he and the clerk were riding south, out of the dark gritstone country into the brighter green fields of the limestone lands.

At Sparrowpit the road improved, being the main highway from Chapel to Stoney Middleton, and the horse, as if appreciative of this fact, quickened its pace. Before long they arrived at the hamlet of Peak Forest, where the clerk reigned in at the doorway of a small tavern.

'Come, boy,' he said. 'Let us have a bite of cheese and a pot of ale before we continue our journey. 'Tis gone noon and I've not broken fast since six o'clock this morn.'

The inn was snug and warm, a comfortable contrast to the air outside, for though all the snow of the past weeks had completely gone the weather was raw and it had proved a cold ride.

Over the meal the clerk became more friendly towards his ward. He had been impressed by the manly way in which Jeremy had taken his misfortune, and he felt a certain sympathy for the boy.

' 'Tis a strange affair to be sure,' he said, between sips of a hot mulled ale the landlord had specially prepared. 'But there's no mending broken pots, they do say. I've no more heart for this business than you have, but the law is the law and must be obeyed.'

'There's no justice in such a cruel law,' Jeremy said bitterly.

'Aye, maybe 'tis so—but laws are made for the common good, and sometimes individuals like yourself get hurt by them. I sometimes think that those who make our laws have never heard of *people*. Perhaps there will come a day when the spirit of the law will count for more than the letter, but such a time has not yet arrived and we can do no more than throw ourselves on the mercy of our betters.'

Jeremy said nothing to this, and after a pause the clerk continued, 'I like you boy—you show uncommon spirit and by your speech, have a smattering of education. This life you are going into—the cotton mill—is a hard one and you will need all your strength and resilience if you are to survive. Take heed of what I say—bend with the storm when it blows, or it will break thee.'

'I don't break easily,' retorted Jeremy with bravado.

'Well, don't say you weren't warned. Bradwell is a hard master and I've heard tales about Cressdale Mill that would make a grown man blanche!'

The mention of the millowner's name brought back to Jeremy the sense of being a victim of some plot and stabbing in the dark, he said, 'It was Bradwell himself who brought my case to the attention of the Poor Law Officers, was it not?'

A spark of appreciation lit the little clerk's eyes, 'Aye, it was—but fancy you knowing that!'

'His son owes me a score and this is how he repays it,' Jeremy answered. Then a new thought struck him. 'But how did he know I was an orphan?'

But that was a question to which the clerk had no answer.

From Peak Forest the highway wound gradually through limestone hills until after about two miles a signpost pointed down a narrower lane to Tideswell. The clerk, familiar with every turn of the countryside hereabouts, took this side-road and before long Jeremy was surprised to see a large village, snugly nestling between folds.

'Tidsell,' announced his companion, using the local name for the place. 'A village hidden from the world at large. They have here a well which ebbs and flows like the sea itself—hence the name: Tide Well.'

From the village the road continued south growing ever narrower and hemmed in by high walls of white limestone. At first it was fairly level going, but then, with an unexpected suddenness, it plunged down a steep, tree-covered hillside.

A few cottages poked from between the trees, and from time to time, where the foliage was thinner Jeremy could look down into a deep valley, narrow like a gorge, flanked by huge white buttresses of limestone. The road was obviously leading into the valley—down, down, now twisting and turning to escape the steep gradient, but still steep enough to make the clerk keep his horse on a tight rein.

At last the road entered a pretty hamlet, set by the stream in the valley bottom. This, the clerk said, was Cressdale, and even as he spoke Jeremy caught his first sight of the mill.

It was not at all what he had expected. He remembered how Sam Ollershaw had once described some mills he had seen—big buildings of bright red brick with hundreds of windows, like some enormous barracks. Cressdale was quite different. It was built of local stone, soft and grey, to a design which resembled a large country house. The central feature was a cobbled millyard entered by an arched gateway as ornamental as any Italian nobleman's palace. On its left was the mill; three storeys high and nobly proportioned—a place of intense activity by the sound of it, for even from a distance Jeremy could hear the metallic clanking of the machines and the muted roar of water over the millwheel.

On the right of the courtyard, facing the mill, was the Factor's cottage and behind that, on a slight eminence, the Apprentice House; a long building of two storeys with mullioned windows.

No expense had been spared to make the mill look attractive. There was even a clock tower with a timepiece coloured in blue enamel and a gilt roof to it, and the gates, too, were gilded. Everything was bright and new and quite beautiful, and when Jeremy saw it he began to wonder whether Cressdale Mill was such a bad place after all.

They rode into the mill yard and dismounted. Leaving Jeremy to hold the horse's bridle, the clerk disappeared into a low building he called the Counting House. In a short while he reappeared with the master of Cressdale, Mr Joshua Bradwell.

Joshua Bradwell had none of the fine clothes or fancy ways of his son, Harrison. He was as short as his son was tall, and running to fat. He was dressed in a plain grey broadcloth even more disreputable than that worn by the clerk, stained on the cuffs and elbow with grease. His red waistcoat was liberally marked with snuff and ale stains and his shirt was of the commonest cotton kind worn by labourers, without cravat. Even his hose was dirty and his shoes had obviously not been cleaned in a twelvemonth.

Whether from infirmity or some youthful accident he had a crook to one shoulder which hunched his head forwards giving him a sinister appearance, and his face, like his clothes, was badly in need of a wash. Jeremy disliked him at once, not only because of his disreputable appearance but because his thin bloodless lips were set in a cruel line and he had evil, glittering eyes, like the eyes of a snake.

When he saw Jeremy he gave a smile which sent a chill into the boy's heart. There was nothing friendly about the smile—it seemed to Jeremy more like the self-satisfied smirk of a man bent on malice.

'Aye, this is t'lad, reet enough,' Bradwell said in a thin, waspish voice. 'Tha's done thi job weel Mester Clerk: here's hafe a guinea for thisel'.'

The little clerk pocketed the money and mounted his horse. 'Take care, boy!' He whispered to Jeremy, that Bradwell might not hear. And he rode away, leaving Jeremy alone with the master of Cressdale Mill.

For a long time Bradwell looked at Jeremy as though he had just bought him in a raffle and wanted to ascertain his quality. His little black eyes missed nothing, and yet he seemed to be puzzled by something. At last he said, 'Ah'm towd that tha caws thisel Jeremy Ollershaw, is that reet?'

'Yes, sir.'

'Is that thi proper name?'

'It is the only name I know, sir.'

Bradwell's eyes narrowed to slits as he considered this reply. It seemed to bother him and he returned to the same question in another way.

'What name did thi parents give thee?'

'That I cannot tell, sir. I lost my memory in a coaching accident and can remember naught of my life before I went to live at Nook Hall. I know nothing of my parents, my true name, nor whence I came.'

Once again that malevolent smile spread across Bradwell's thin lips, as though the boy's misfortune was some enormous joke. Jeremy could have hit him, but remembering what the clerk had said, he kept his anger under control.

'Well, Mester Jeremy Ollershaw, tha's now a 'prentice at Cressdale Mill,' said Bradwell, with obvious satisfaction in his voice. 'Ah've heerd tales on thee from my son Harrison, and by aw accounts theer's a lot o' wickedness and ungodliness in thee as needs curbin'. A young devil, so folk say. Pity—'cos if theer's one thing I cawn't abide, it's wickedness in young folk!'

Jeremy's face flushed scarlet at these montrous lies. 'I assure you, sir . . .' he began, but got no further. Bradwell lifted a foot and kicked him hard in the stomach. With a groan, Jeremy sank to the cobbles. His head swam with coloured lights and he felt like retching.

'Speak when tha spokken to!' ordered Bradwell. 'Now get up an' follow me.'

Inside the mill the noise was deafening. Huge machines the like of which Jeremy had never seen before, clanked and rattled in perpetual motion like metallic demons driven by the ceaselessy churning water wheel. Men and boys moved amongst the machinery, lugging heavy bales of new cotton, or carrying baskets of bobbins with partly spun thread. Exactly what was happening was beyond Jeremy's grasp, but he could see that the raw cotton bales were being broken open and the fluffy material inside was being straightened out and pulled into long hanks. Later, he came to know a good deal about carding, twisting and spinning.

The ground floor of the mill; mostly consisted of a bare, cold, stone flagged barracks with rough stone walls and strong iron pillars set at regular intervals to support the upper floors. These pillars were very necessary, as Jeremy quickly discovered when he followed Bradwell up the steep stairs, for the upper floors were crammed with spinning frames, the combined weight of which must have been many tons.

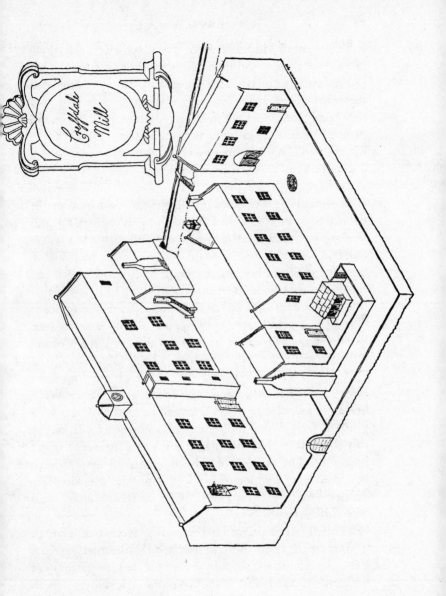

Coffdale Mill

The main driving shaft from the water wheel ran along one side of the ground-floor room and from it strong ropes in the form of pulleys went up to drive the machinery on the other floors. Here the noise was different but equally deafening; an incessant clacking as though a thousand little gnomes were tapping with hammers. It was caused by the whirling bobbins of the spinning frames where gossamer threads were being spun into the finished product.

To Jeremy it was a strange, frightening world after the peacefulness of Nook Hall. Everything and everyone was moving in frenzied haste, and noise and bustle was without end. Cotton was everywhere: bales of it, hanks of it, bobbins of it. It lay on the floor in dropped tufts and rejected waste ends, it even floated in the air as minute fibres which caught in one's throat. Jeremy wondered that such a small fibre could cause all this activity—no wonder Sam Ollershaw had once called it King Cotton. It was a soft thread with an iron rule!

If Jeremy was overawed by the machinery and the noise he did not fail to notice his fellow apprentices. What he saw was not encouraging: thin, ragged children with pinched faces, some only seven or eight years old and so tiny that they had to stand on stools to reach their machines. The boys wore only shirt and trousers, though the mill was damp and cold, the girls plain, pinafore dresses. All were barefoot, with unkempt hair, and incredibly dirty.

Though these things in themselves were bad enough it was the faces of the children which alarmed Jeremy. Pale, sickly, their faces had set into a look of permanent resignation, hard and without emotion, and eyes which reflected utter hopelessness. He felt a cold chill of apprehension to think that these were his companions of the future and he wondered whether he too would become like them.

When finally they reached the top floor, Bradwell called one of the overseers.

'A new 'prentice for thee, Jem,' he said. 'The very same as our Harrison towd us on.'

'Oh, aye,' replied the overseer, looking at Jeremy with interest. He was a big man—well over six foot—and broad to match. He had an evil, pock-marked face which lent him a brutal look. 'I heerd Mester Harrison say as how he were a reet wicked lad—happen we'll learn him better! What's thi name, young 'un?'

'Jeremy Ollershaw,' the boy replied. The next instant he received a stinging blow to the side of the head which sent him sprawling on the filthy floor. The giant overseer bent and lifted him to his feet with one hand. Thrusting his ugly face close to Jeremy's he snarled, 'Tha caws me *Mester Marsh* when tha speaks to me, brat, an' doant thee forget it!'

Bradwell laughed. 'That'll tak some o' thi steam away,' he said. 'If he gives thi ony moor trouble, Jem, belt t'livin' dayleets out o'un! He's a big lad, too, so put him on heavy work.'

Jeremy never worked so hard as he did in the next four hours. Following the mill owner's instructions he was put to work on the hoist, pulling up the heavy bales of raw cotton from the yard.

The hoist consisted of a doorway over which projected a wooden beam equipped with a pulley wheel. A rope ran over the wheel from the doorway down to ground level, and by means of this simple device, the cotton bales could be raised to the top floor of the mill from the yard.

The bales of cotton were very heavy and it took all Jeremy's strength to prevent the weight from snatching the rope out of his grasp. As he heaved and sweated the thick cord chafed his palms until they were raw, but when he complained to Jem Marsh his only reply was a cuff on the ear and a stern warning not to slacken work. There was nothing Jeremy could do but pull and strain until his back ached and his arms felt ready to drop off.

He had, however, plenty of time to think, and when he thought of the fact that he was condemned to Cressdale Mill for the next seven years he felt very bitter towards those who had put him there. Why was Bradwell so obviously against him? Perhaps one day he would find out.

At first Jeremy thought that the overseer, Marsh, had singled him out for particularly hard treatment but he soon found that his lot was no worse than the other apprentices. Marsh was a natural bully; a man who took sadistic pleasure in kicking and beating the young boys and girls in his charge, often for no reason at all. Strangely enough, they seemed to expect this savage treatment, and one or two would curse and swear at the overseer in the vilest language, but he would just laugh or give them another cuff.

When darkness fell large tallow candles were lit in wall niches and the work went on as before. The flickering light threw shadows of strange half-human forms on the bare walls, and Cressdale Mill looked more than ever like a workshop in Hell.

At seven o'clock a bell rang from the mill yard and the great waterwheel which provided the power for all this industry clanked to a stop.

Jeremy felt like dropping to the floor from sheer exhaustion. Suddenly he was aware of the huge bulk of the overseer standing over him.

'Works o'er,' Marsh announced. 'Now's when us has us victuals and play!' Turning to the other youngsters he cried, 'Coom and meet thi new workmate!'

The ragged crew gathered round obediently and from their giggling and sly nudges it was apparent that they expected Marsh to be up to some sport. They were not disappointed.

'Let's see thi hands, lad,' the overseer demanded of Jeremy.

Obediently the boy held out his palms, revealing them sore and raw. A gasp went up from the others.

'Deary me!' exclaimed the overseer, in mock horror. 'Tha's been howdin' on to t'rope aw wrong. Tha mun howd it like this, sithee.' And he grasped the rope in his great fists. Jeremy could see no difference.

'Tell thi what—thee get howd on t'other end; one as t'cotton is raised on.'

A sixth sense told Jeremy that Marsh was up to some trick, that he was not to be trusted, but he had to do what the overseer bid. Drawing in the other end of the rope he gripped it firmly, clenching his teeth over the soreness of his hands.

No sooner had he got a firm hold than Marsh gave him a quick shove through the hoist doorway and sent him penduling over space, three floors above the mill yard!

As all his weight came on to his raw hands Jeremy gave a cry of pain. It was all he could do to hold on, though he knew that if he should let go he would be maimed for life or even killed.

Marsh and the apprentices thought it was a huge joke; they laughed and applauded as Jeremy spiralled on the rope, fighting for his life.

The overseer pretended to reach out from the door and

save Jeremy and his grotesque efforts made the other apprentices howl with delight like a pack of bloodthirsty young wolves. So insensitive had they become to pain that their only pleasure in life was to see others suffer like themselves.

'I cawn't seem to reach thee, lad—tha'll hev for t'climb down t'rope,' Marsh shouted to the despairing Jeremy.

'I can't,' gasped the boy. 'My hands—.'

'Tha's getten sore hands reet enough,' agreed the overseer, 'but if tha lets goo tha'll hev a sore heed!' This was considered a masterpiece of wit by the children who laughed loudly. 'Tell thi what—we'll walk down and catch thee!'

With this Marsh and the others withdrew, leaving Jeremy hanging from the rope.

He was glad that it was dark—at least he could not see the cobblestones of the millyard, though he was conscious that they were waiting for him should he slip. His arms were lead, his hands smarted, and something like panic gripped him as he realised that he would not be able to hang on to the rope much longer.

Suddenly, something snapped in his brain. A great surge of action swept through him; a determination to survive. He told himself to climb down the rope as sailors did, using his legs to take the strain off his arms. Instantly he put the thought to work and within two minutes he reached the ground safely.

He leant against the mill wall feeling sick with relief and his mind began to turn towards thoughts of escape. So consumed was he by his desire to get away that he did not stop to wonder how he knew of the way sailors climbed ropes.

CHAPTER FOUR

ESCAPE!

THE LIGHTS OF the Apprentice House threw a warm glow across the cobbled mill yard, reminding Jeremy that it was hours since he had last eaten.

A noisy group of youngsters were making their way towards the building, so Jeremy followed them, hoping they would lead him to his supper and a bed for the night. Nobody had told Jeremy where he was to eat or sleep, but on enquiry from one of the boys, he was informed that Old Moses Gault, the Apprentice Master, would see him right.

'But get your supper first, mate,' his informant added in a strong Cockney accent, 'or there won't be none left, see?'

The entrance to the Apprentice House was through a narrow doorway which led directly into the main dining hall. Despite its low ceiling the room had the atmosphere of a barn, with unplastered stone walls, narrow windows and a flagged floor. At the end nearest the door a flight of stone steps led to the upper storey where the apprentices slept and at the far end there was a serving hatch presided over by a blowsy dame intent on ladling out some kind of soup. In between, the floor space was occupied with long trestle tables and benches at which fifty or sixty apprentices of all ages were noisily eating supper.

The din was appalling, and the stench, compounded of stale cooking and unwashed bodies, even more so. To

Jeremy it seemed as though he had entered a den of thieves or gipsies except that these were all children.

Some of the younger children lay sprawled across the tables, white faced and head in hands, as though exhausted by the day's labour. The older ones talked and joked at the tops of their voices, banging the tables with their fists and occasionally punching each other. Over in one corner he noticed a boy and girl screaming abuse at one another over the ownership of a piece of bread.

Jeremy pushed his way through the crowded room to the serving hatch, where the greasy old woman, who turned out to be Mrs Gault, the Apprentice Master's wife, appraised him and said, 'Ah've noan seed thee afore.'

'I came this day, ma'am,' replied Jeremy.

Mother Gault shrugged. 'Well, here's thi supper,' she said, handing him a plate. 'Tha'll find a bed upstairs when thas ready for yon—and that'll be soon enough I warrant!'

Jeremy found an empty place at a table. Hungry though he was, the meal looked far from appetising; a sort of watery cabbage soup in which floated a piece of fatty bacon. A large hunk of stale bread accompanied this meal, and since neither knife nor spoon was provided, Jeremy dipped the bread in the broth and chewed on it.

He almost choked on the first mouthful. Never in his life had he tasted anything so foul. From the place next to him came a quiet laugh and turning, Jeremy saw that he was being watched by a thin little urchin, with sharp eyes and dark hair. The boy was perhaps eleven years old, though very small, and he gave Jeremy an encouraging grin.

' 'Tis the fish wot does it, mate,' said the urchin cheerfully, pointing a grubby finger at the food. He had the same strange London accent of many of the other boys.

'The fish?' Jeremy said.

'Yus. Old Bradwell—God damn 'is soul—buys cheap Irish bacon; pigs fed on fish meal, see? Taste's 'orrible, don't it?'

'I can't eat it,' agreed Jeremy with disgust.

The other sighed philosophically. 'That's wot they all says at first, but starvation's a wonderful leveller, mark my words. A few days in this 'ole an' you'll eat anyfink! 'Ere—if you don't want it, give it to me!'

Jeremy pushed the nauseating bowl over to his new-found friend, who scooped out the bacon with one grubby paw as though it was a prize to be treasured. He polished it off like a seal eating mackerel, and with equal facility disposed of the cabbage soup. When every morsel was gone he beamed with pleasure, as though he had just had the treat of his young life.

'What's your name, mate?' he demanded in the perky manner which Jeremy began to like.

'Jeremy Ollershaw.'

'Mine's Joe Walls—though everyone calls me Little Joey, 'cos I'm a bit of a runt, see? I'm eleven years old an' I been in this hell-hole for eighteen months. How old are you?'

'Fourteen.'

'Lucky devil!' exclaimed Joey with envy. 'That means you only got seven years to do—me, I got another ten. Allus supposin' I lives that long, mark you.'

'Come now, Joey!' Jeremy cried. 'Don't talk like that. It's—well, it's like tempting Providence!'

'I reckon we all tempts Providence every day in this place,' Joey replied bitterly. 'You don't know the half of it, mate. Eighteen months ago there was ten of us came from Clerkenwell Poor House, and how many are there now, I might arsk? Eight, mate—'cos two of em are in Tideswell Churchyard, six feet below the sod!'

Jeremy was shocked by this startling piece of news, and yet, as he looked around at the miserable wretches who were to be his workmates, he found it easy to believe. All of them, boys and girls alike, were emaciated, tired and broken. They fought and they quarrelled, they laughed and shouted, but there was no light shining in their eyes, only a dull hopelessness. Some were obviously ill and in need of medical attention, but at Cressdale Mill, such a thing was a luxury—if you could stand, you worked. It was hard to believe that these boys and girls were human beings at all, so low had they sunk in bodily health and personal cleanliness, and there and then Jeremy decided that no matter what happened he would never become like one of them: he would fight back in every possible way.

Somehow, Little Joey seemed different from the others. True, he was frail and thin, incredibly grubby and given to using oaths whenever he spoke, but at least he still had spirit; indeed, he seemed positively cheerful. He told Jeremy all about his journey from London in a covered cart—most of the mill apprentices came from London Poor Houses it seemed—and how full of hope they had all been for a new life. They had been promised all sorts of good things, and on the journey they had even been given a whole shilling for spending on apples and sweets at Nottingham Market, but they were very quickly disillusioned once they reached Cressdale. Their indentures were worthless scraps of paper, binding on them but not on their employer, with the result that their 'apprentice-ship' consisted of nothing but drudgery for twelve to fourteen hours a day. Sunday was the day of rest, but to earn it they worked until midnight on Saturday—an eighteen hour day.

Sometimes, on Bradwell's orders, Old Moses Gault paraded them all to church on a Sunday, and this was their religious education. They also received wages of a sort—but there were so many fines for bad workmanship that more often than not the fines and the wages cancelled each other, and they were no better off.

As Little Joey talked Jeremy had the weird feeling that he had heard it all before, but not about Cressdale, about some far distant place . . . He could see in his mind's eye rows of pathetic black faces—slaves! That was it, slaves! But try as he would he could not understand why he should think of slaves, or how he came to know of such things.

'But how can such cruelties exist?' he demanded at last. 'Surely this is not the Law? Are we not supposed to be protected by the Justices?'

Joey snorted his contempt for the Justices. ''Course it's not the Law,' he agreed. 'An' the Justices come visitin' from time to time, but what happens, I arsk yer? Old Bradwell, damn his soul, treats 'em to a feast and lots of port an' they never gets round to seein' *us*.'

The more Little Joey talked, the more convinced did Jeremy become that he was in a trap for life; a trap where the ordinary rules of justice did not apply, where the masters could do no wrong and where their helpless child victims had no redress. Jeremy wanted no part of it. He felt a sudden hate for Bradwell and his kind surging up inside him. He felt as though he had to get away, to tell the world about the cruel conditions in which mill children lived.

Lowering his voice he asked whether there were no escapes.

'Lots o' times,' answered the little Cockney cheerfully. 'But where can they run to? They ain't got no homes, have they? They nearly allus comes back—an' then they gets a beatin' for their trouble. 'Ere—you aint finkin' of runnin' away already, are you?'

'Why not?' demanded Jeremy stoutly. ''Tis best to get away while I still have some strength left.'

'There's truth enough in that,' Joey agreed.

'I shall go—tonight.'

Joey gave a low whistle of surprise. 'In the *dark?*' he asked incredulously. 'You can't go at night, mate. Why, there's all sorts o' wild animals out on them moors at night. Bears and wolves, so I've heard tell—an' worse than that, there's evil spirits!'

'Tosh! That's old wives' talk, Joey. I've been on the moors at night. There's only the weather to worry about, and tonight may be cold but at least it is fine. I'll survive, never fear!'

To a Londoner born and bred like Little Joey, the thought of venturing into wild open country late at night seemed verging on madness. Nevertheless, he had a strong admiration for this dark handsome boy with the determined face and he felt that if anyone could do it, then Jeremy was the one.

Dropping his voice to a conspiratorial whisper he said, 'Moses Gault locks the doors of the 'prentice house as soon as everyone's gone to bed—which is in about five minutes from now, by my reckonin'. Then in about half an hour he comes upstairs to see that everyone is asleep. After that, the coast is clear, mate!'

'But how do I get out?'

'There's a window at the top o' the landin' by the stairs. It looks on to the Factor's yard an' below the window there's a pig stye . . .'

'Then I can drop from the window on to the pig stye roof!'

' 'Sright, only the Factor happens to keep two large mastiffs chained in the yard—nasty brutes an' all, they are. If they sniffs yer, you're done for.'

'That's a risk I'll have to take,' said Jeremy stoutly. 'What comes next?'

'There's the wall of the yard to be scaled, and then the wall of the mill yard. Beyond that there's plenty o' trees for cover.'

Jeremy looked at the little Londoner. 'Then I'm game,' he said. 'Will you come with me?'

Joey smiled wistfully. 'Not me, mate,' he said sadly, and stood up. To Jeremy's horror he saw that one of the boy's legs was completely crippled.

'I'm sorry—I didn't know . . .' Jeremy stammered.

'That's all right, mate. Come away upstairs and I'll find you a bunk where you can rest for a while until you're good and ready.'

Together they climbed the steep stone steps to the apprentice dormitories. At the head of the stairs, dimly lit by a single candle, Jeremy could see a long corridor running the length of the building. At the end nearest the stairs a door led into the boys' dormitory and at the far end a similar door led to the girls' sleeping quarters. At the very point where the stairs met the landing, Jeremy noticed the window which Little Joey had mentioned and he was satisfied that though it was narrow he would be able to squeeze through.

They were the last to enter the dormitory, which was

3

dark and overcrowded with two-tiered bunks. It smelt abominably of stale air and dirt. Joey found an empty bunk near the door, where Jeremy could lie in wait and then slip out easily when Moses Gault had done his rounds.

'Good luck, mate,' he whispered. 'I hopes yer makes it.'

Jeremy took the little boy's hand and pressed it warmly.

'Thanks for all your help, Joey. I'll not forget you.'

'Well, that's somefink, anyway,' said Joey with a grin, and he vanished into the dark interior of the room.

Jeremy undressed and lay on the cot with a blanket pulled round him. It was cold in the dormitory but he was so tired after his long day that he would have fallen asleep had he not deliberately kept himself awake with the prospect of his escape. The only sound from the other apprentices was that of heavy breathing and occasional snores.

It seemed as though Old Gault would never come, and once or twice the notion crossed Jeremy's mind that the Apprentice Master was missing his duty for the evening. But at last the shuffling of footsteps on the stone stair, a chink of candlelight, and a muttered cursing told him that Gault was on his rounds.

Obviously the old man found the steep stairs something of a problem, for it took him a long time to climb them, with several pauses for breath. Jeremy half closed his eyes and waited.

At last the door of the dormitory was opened and by squinting through his half closed lids Jeremy could see the fat jowls of the Apprentice Master and his heavy body, framed against the candlelight. He held his breath. Gault, however, seemed in no mood for a close examination of the room's occupants, but just stood for a moment in the

doorway, then turned round and made his way downstairs.

When at last the sound of Gault's footsteps had died
away, Jeremy slid noiselessly from beneath his blanket and
dressed quickly. His feet felt cold on the bare floor but
he dare not wear his clogs, which he stuffed as an awkward
bundle down his shirt front.

As he opened the door it creaked on its hinges and
Jeremy paused, chill fingers of fear running up his spine.
Had he wakened anyone? Only the heavy breathing of
tired bodies disturbed the darkness.

Out on the landing he quickly slipped the window
catch and opening the casement, peered down.

A silver winter's moon bathed the mill in a ghostly
glow and nothing living stirred. It was just as Joey had
described it—the pig stye lay immediately below the
window in a large private yard belonging to the Factor.
This in turn was bounded by a high stone wall and there
was another wall beyond. Then there were trees and
freedom.

To Jeremy, the drop from the window to the roof of
the stye seemed pretty formidable at first, but he reckoned
that if he hung from the windowsill by the tips of his
fingers he would not have more than three or four feet
to fall. Fortunately, the strong gritstone flags of the stye
roof would easily bear his weight.

He was surprised at the force of his landing. His bare
feet slapped hard against the cold flags, his knees buckled,
and he rolled uncontrollably down the steep pitch of the
roof into the pig stye.

As he clattered down the roof he heard the dogs begin
barking and a light went on at the rear of the Factor's
House. Angry voices sounded and Jeremy, thoroughly

alarmed, crawled into the pig stye and hid between the wall and the warm flanks of a big fat sow. The sow gave a grunt, then ignored him.

The back door of the house was flung open with a crash and Jeremy heard the harsh clatter of clogs on the cobbled yard.

'Damn them dogs!' A loud voice cried angrily. 'Ah'll shoot yon brutes one o' these fine neets, see if I doan't!'

A light, dancing from a hand lantern, swung crazy beams round the yard. Jeremy crouched low.

'Theer's nowt amiss, tha silly besoms!' The voice continued, obviously speaking to the barking dogs. 'Howd thi racket, afore tha waks up aw t'mill!' And with a curse the voice's owner went back inside the house.

Whether reassured by their master's voice or cowed by his temper, the dogs stopped barking and Jeremy breathed easier. After a moment of hesitation he crawled out of the stye and began scaling the wall, thankful at the roughness of the stones which made climbing easy. Five minutes later he reached the woods.

For a long time Jeremy just lay in the woods, feeling a sense of excitement and freedom and trying to think what course of action he should next adopt. To go running to Nook Hall by the way he had come would be suicidal, he decided, because that is exactly what Bradwell would expect him to do, and Jeremy had no intention of being caught so easily. Better to take his time, to work round in an arc so as to fetch up at Nook Hall in three or four days, when the hue and cry had died down.

The thought of Nook Hall and the Ollershaws brought a lump to Jeremy's throat. How he missed them! It was incredible to think that it was less than twenty-four hours since he lived there, seemingly safe and secure. Already it seemed half a lifetime ago. In his mind's eye he pictured the kitchen and the roaring fire at Nook Hall, and he shivered involuntarily as the cold night air of the woods cut through his thin shirt.

One thing was sure—he could not remain in the woods. They were much too near the mill. By dawn he wanted to be well clear of Cressdale.

The woods were not thick and being winter the trees were bare of leaves so that pale moonlight filtered down between the interlaced branches making it easy for Jeremy to find his way. Twigs snapped underfoot with disconcerting loudness and his clogs clattered against loose stones with a noise fit to wake the whole village, but nobody seemed to hear. Once or twice Jeremy started as a nocturnal fox or badger made a movement in the dark undergrowth.

A deep side-valley, well wooded, cut away from the main dale in a northerly direction and Jeremy decided to follow it. It offered shelter and at the same time provided a way out of Cressdale not taken by any road.

In the bottom of the valley ran a stony brook which glittered like a silver snake in the moonlight. Jeremy followed its course for a short distance until he came upon a narrow path meandering through the woods in the direction of the valley head. About ten minutes after he had joined this path the woods fell back in an open glade and the clearing of the trees allowed Jeremy to see for the first time the precipitous sides of his little valley. To his left steeply wooded slopes ran up towards the Tideswell road, but on his right the valley was lined by magnificent limestone crags. Bathed in moonlight, the white crags were awe inspiring—at least two hundred feet—and absolutely precipitous. One crag especially drew Jeremy's attention; a huge bastion like the keep of some giant's castle.

Jeremy was held spellbound by the beauty of it all and he felt drawn towards the majestic cliffs. He recalled how during his terrible ordeal in the Winnat's Pass the cliffs there had given him shelter and it seemed likely that these too might have a cave where he could spend the night.

It was a long steep pull up loose limestone scree to the foot of the crags, but it was not labour in vain. A little way along the crag Jeremy came upon a fantastic flying buttress of rock which jutted out from the main cliff and through which Nature had hollowed out a tunnel to form a wonderfully dry and sheltered cave. Tired and hungry, Jeremy soon found a comfortable niche and fell soundly asleep.

When he awoke next morning there was a rime on the rocks but the sky was blue and clear. From the mouth of his cave he could look down on a wonderful panorama which took in the length of his little valley and beyond it to Cressdale Mill, so distant that it appeared no more than a toy. He wondered what Bradwell was doing about his escape—it was certain to have been discovered by this time.

At first Jeremy thought of remaining in the cave until nightfall, and then continuing his journey under the cover of darkness, but he felt cold and very hungry and he had the sense to realise that he must obtain food if he was to survive at all, much less reach Nook Hall. There was nothing for it but to risk travelling by day.

He followed the line of the white crags until bit by bit they diminished in height and eventually merged into smooth grassy slopes. The valley had become bowl-shaped, treeless and criss-crossed with neat limestone walls forming fields in which flocks of fat sheep grazed contentedly. So hungry was Jeremy that he thought of killing a sheep for food, but a moment's reflection warned him that sheep stealing was a very serious crime, for which the punishment would certainly be transportation for life, or even hanging. Hungry though he was, this sombre thought was enough to put the idea out of his head immediately.

In a little while he came across a green lane, like a drovers' road, bounded on either side by the inevitable limestone walls, which crawled steeply up the side of the valley until it met with a miry cart-road, where a boundary stone of lichenous antiquity told Jeremy he was entering the hamlet of Wardlow.

The road descended a slight brow and Jeremy could see the widely scattered cottages and farmhouses of the place. There was no focal point—no church or large mansion for the village to nestle by—but there was an inn, and an inn meant food. A farmer's cart trundled up the hill, but apart from this and a woman carrying a bundle of faggots on her shoulder, Wardlow seemed deserted, and Jeremy reckoned he would be quite safe to try his luck there.

In his pocket he still had the four pennies he had been given the day he met Mr Mendoza in Chapel en le Frith and jingling these merrily he strode towards the weather-beaten sign of a *Bull's Head*. Two pence should see him fed, he thought, and the idea of sitting by a nice warm fire as well spurred him on.

A narrow door led into the inn. Inside, Jeremy found a low beamed room, mellowed by smoke and warmed by a glowing coal fire. There was only one other customer, a young man dressed in neat but plain broadcloth and wearing a tricorne hat, sitting on a settle by the fire, sipping ale from a pewter tankard.

Opposite the fireplace a sort of counter served as a bar and behind it a buxom woman, in her middle fifties, stood plucking a chicken. She stared at Jeremy suspiciously as he entered.

'An' what might thee be wantin', young 'un?' she asked, holding the chicken up by its scraggy neck and inspecting her handiwork.

'Bread and cheese, if you please, ma'am—and a mug of mulled ale,' Jeremy replied.

The landlady put down the chicken and wiped her hands on her pinny, 'Oh aye? Victuals and ale costs brass, lad—has tha getten ony?'

Jeremy placed two pennies on the bar. Scooping them up the woman put the coins in her apron pocket and disappeared through a curtain into the back room.

'Tha looks reet cowd, young sir,' said the man by the fire in a high piping voice. 'Coom an' sit thisel' by t'fire.'

Jeremy was glad of the invitation. His night out had starved his body and the warm fire felt luxurious. He thanked the stranger. The man's thin sallow face gave a weak smile.

' 'Tis a mite early for thi jackbit,' the stranger said, as the landlady reappeared with Jeremy's meal.

'I have not yet eaten this morning,' said Jeremy, shortly. He attacked the bread and cheese ravenously.

'So, 'twould seem,' the man observed, drily. 'Hast coom far, then?'

'No,' answered Jeremy, not at all liking the way the stranger was inquisitive. 'What about you, sir? Have you travelled far?' He parried.

'Fra Bakewell wi' a suit o' clothes for a local farmer,' the young man replied. 'Ma name's Sam French; journeyman tailor. Theer's them as says ah cuts t'best broadcloth i' aw t'North o' England.'

'An' theer's a lot moor as says tha doesn't,' the landlady called, interrupting the conversation.

French turned and shouted, 'Then a plague on 'em— an' a plague on thee, too, Betsy Standish.' He apologised to Jeremy for the break in conversation. 'Times are hard, young sir, reet hard, an' it's bad enough folk not payin' their bills wi'out havin' tavern wenches run down thi' good name!'

For about half an hour they talked together, mostly the tailor telling Jeremy about his trade and how lots of people owed him money, and what bad luck he had had in general. Jeremy found the young man pleasant enough but he could not help thinking that he was not a very good tailor, or he would have more custom and could not afford to idle away the morning talking to strangers.

The warmth of the fire, the food and hot mulled ale considerably revived Jeremy and his mind turned again to his journey. As he made ready to go, however, the tailor detained him.

'Nay, lad,' said Sam French in protest. 'One mug o' ale is nowt on a cowd day like yon—tha mun have another wi' me. Betsy—another pot o' ale for t'young 'un!'

There was little use in protesting, so Jeremy thanked the tailor. French drew from his pocket a twist of paper which he unscrewed to reveal some grains of powder. 'Now this *really* keeps t'cowd out o' thi bones,' he said. ' 'Tis a secret potion made by mi' owd granny from a gypsy remedy. It stops thi havin' ague an' rheum an' aw manner o' ills.'

3*

Betsy fetched the ale and French tipped the potion into it. 'Sup up, lad,' he said cheerfully.

Jeremy lifted the pot and took a strong draught of the hot liquid. The potion made it taste bitter, but if it did prevent ills, as the tailor claimed, then he was grateful—the last thing he wanted was to be ill on his escape. He downed the drink manfully.

'Thank you again, sir, and now I must be on my way,' he said, rising to his feet.

Suddenly, his knees went weak and buckled beneath him. The room seemed to go whirling round like a top and he gripped the settle back for support. He had a momentary vision of the little tailor grinning at him. Then he blacked out.

CHAPTER FIVE

CRESSDALE MILL

A BUCKET OF ice-cold water thrown over his face roused Jeremy from a deep, deep sleep. It felt like coming out of a long dark tunnel—for a minute or two his confused mind struggled to regain consciousness, then, little by little, things became clearer. His head ached dully and he longed to go back to sleep, but another bucket of water put paid to that idea. He shook his head and opened his eyes.

He found himself lying on the cobbles of the mill yard at Cressdale, his hands securely tied behind his back. Joshua Bradwell and the little tailor stood looking down at him.

'Theer! An' what did I tell thee, Mester Bradwell?' the tailor exclaimed on seeing Jeremy open his eyes. 'He's noan deed after aw!'

'Tha'll goo too far one o' these fine days, Sam French,' the mill owner replied sharply. 'Laudanum's a pison, tha knows!'

The tailor smirked. 'Nay, Mester Bradwell—a drop o' laudanum ne'er did onybody much harm. It just knocks 'em out cowd for a few hours!' Turning to Jeremy he said cheerfully, 'Hey up, young 'un! Art aw reet? Tha's a bonny 'un tryin' to run away fro' thi mester!'

'How did you guess?' Jeremy groaned.

'It were noan a guess, lad,' the tailor replied. 'Ah' seen too mony o' thy sort not for t'recognize one!'

Jeremy realised how he had been completely duped by

the little tailor, who must have known all along that he was a runaway apprentice, almost certainly from Cressdale. He felt sick at the thought of how friendly the tailor had pretended to be, and he felt ashamed of himself for falling for the trick of allowing the man to put knock-out drops in his ale. Herbs, he had called them—some herbs!

What puzzled Jeremy was why the tailor should go to so much trouble over an escaped apprentice, but this was quickly resolved when he saw Bradwell hand over five shillings.

'Theer's thi bounty,' said Bradwell with ill grace, as though he was loth to part with the money. 'Five good shillings—that's t'regular price for runaway 'prentices.'

'Thank'ee, Mester Bradwell,' said the tailor, pocketing the money and touching his tricorne hat obsequiously. 'Ony time I con be of service—' Bradwell dismissed him with a wave of his hand, and the tailor strode off, whistling a tune at his good fortune.

Bradwell looked down at the helpless Jeremy with smouldering malice in his eyes. 'So tha'd try an' run away, would tha?' he growled. 'Tha's getten a lot for t'learn, young 'un, an' we mun try for t'curb thi high spirits.'

Jem Marsh had been standing close by, still holding the bucket whose contents he had poured over Jeremy. At a signal from Bradwell the overseer came forward, at the same time unbuckling a thick leather belt from round his waist. His face twisted into a sadistic grin. He wrapped the buckle end of the belt tightly round one of his enormous fists, leaving the other to swing ominously.

'Ah'll leave thee to it, Jem,' said Bradwell. 'Tha knows what for t'do, reet enough.' With a final look of hate at Jeremy he took himself off.

Marsh stood over his helpless victim.

'Tha's bin a nowty lad, Jeremy,' he said in that mocking tone which Jeremy knew was a warning sign. 'Tha mun be punished. Ah'm gooin' for t'give thee a reet good flankin' lad!'

Marsh was as good as his word. For fifteen minutes he flayed Jeremy with the leather belt until the boy's arms, legs and even his face, was a red mass of contusions. All the overseer's considerable strength went into the blows and it was as if he was trying not only to inflict pain but break Jeremy's spirit as well.

But Jeremy was equally determined not to be broken. Though each succeeding blow hurt more than the last, he bit his lips against crying out.

At last Marsh, exhausted by his own efforts, put the belt round his waist again. Untying Jeremy, he dragged him on to his feet. Dazed and sore, the boy still had enough spirit left to stand upright and look the cruel overseer straight in the face. As if it was some kind of Fate which stared at him, Marsh suddenly averted his eyes. He had beaten the lad blue—yet he had not broken him.

'Ah'll say this much for thee, young 'un,' he muttered. 'Tha's getten courage. Theer's very few as could have takken such a flankin' wi'out skrikin'.'

There was even a hint of admiration in the overseer's voice, for like many of his kind, though without normal pity or compassion, and cruel to a degree, he recognized courage when he saw it. It was like flint striking steel; it struck a spark of appreciation—perhaps the only sort of appreciation which Marsh and his kind were capable of experiencing. He had no cause to dislike Jeremy in the first place—if he was cruel to him, so he was to all the apprentices—and now the boy's courage made him feel favourably disposed towards him.

'Get thisel' weshed,' he said gruffly. 'Ah reckon tha's had enough for one day. Tha con lie on thi bunk an' Ah'll tell t'mester as how tha be too bad for t'work.'

But Jeremy shook his head stubbornly. 'I want no favours, Jem Marsh,' he said evenly. 'I will work!'

His body ached all over and he would dearly have loved to take up the overseer's offer of a rest, but he had no intention of being indebted to anybody at Cressdale Mill.

Marsh was astounded. In all his years' experience he had never heard anybody refuse time off. The offer itself was as rare as snow in June—but to have it refused! He looked at Jeremy to reassure himself that this unusual lad really was an apprentice. He saw a strong, dark haired boy, bigger than average perhaps, but not uncommon. He was like a hundred other lads of his age. What disturbed Marsh, however, was the firm set of Jeremy's face; cool, level eyes and a strong, determined jaw. Not only was this boy tough and resilient, he had a will of iron.

Marsh was nobody's fool. He recognized at once that though he might kill Jeremy, he could never break him, and so, like all bullies, he decided to leave well enough alone.

'Work if tha must,' he said gruffly, adding, 'Th'art a hard lad, reet enough. By gum, but th'art a hard lad!' And without another word he strode off into the mill.

Jeremy followed him into the noisy building, up the stairs. A group of apprentices seeing them approach and noticing Jeremy's bruised appearance let out animal like howls of derision. One youth, seeking to toady favour with the overseer, danced in front of Jeremy, taunting him.

'See what we got here, mates!' he cried gloatingly. 'A runaway 'prentice, no less! You'll suffer for that, me bucko—ain't that so, Mr Marsh?'

But Marsh fetched him a clout across the ear which stopped him dead and he looked like a spaniel struck by its master; hurt and puzzled. The others, too, became subdued.

'Get back to thi work!' Marsh growled. 'He's getten moor spunk than aw on yo lot put together!'

When Jeremy heard that, a strange feeling swelled up inside him; a mixture of joy and savage satisfaction. Young though he was he realised that he had broken Marsh; that never again would the cruel overseer try beating him!

That evening, as Jeremy entered the dining hall, a hush fell on the assembled apprentices. News of his escape and recapture had quickly gone the rounds, and the story of his savage beating had been the talk of the mill. The tale had lost nothing in the telling, either—it was whispered that Marsh had beaten him for an hour without so much as making him cry, until in the end it was the overseer who collapsed with sheer exhaustion!

And so Jeremy, much to his surprise and embarrassment, found himself the hero of the hour, with everyone crowding forward to get a good look at him. One figure detached itself from the rest and came forward to grip his hand.

'Bad luck gettin' caught like that, mate,' said Little Joey, with his usual cheeky grin. 'Reckon' I should have warned thee about bounty seekers.'

Jeremy was glad to see the little Londoner again. ' 'Tis not your fault, Joey,' he replied. 'He would never have caught me had he not put laudanum in my ale.'

Cries of shame went up at this tit-bit of information, for the crowd were hanging on to every word, and someone ventured the opinion that all bounty seekers should swing. This was universally approved of and then Jeremy was made to recount his adventures in detail while the older apprentices nodded approval and the younger ones sat wide-eyed with the wonder of it all.

Supper had been forgotten in the excitement of the story-telling but when at last it was all over and Jeremy made his way to the serving hatch he found that Mother Gault had been listening too. She was wiping tears from her eyes.

'Ee, tha poor lad,' she clucked sympathetically. 'Tha's had thi share o' trouble an' no mistake—but tha tells a tale beautifully!'

'And now I'm hungry, Mrs Gault,' Jeremy replied. 'Though I never thought I'd be glad to eat Irish bacon.'

Mother Gault winked at him. 'I allus keeps summat special back,' she said. 'What would tha say to some nice mutton chops, eh?'

'And what about my friend Joey?' asked Jeremy, his mouth watering at the thought of fresh meat.

'Theer's plenty for both on thee,' said Mother Gault.

Little Joey's grin went wider than ever. 'Fings is certainly lookin' up, mate!' he observed, philosophically.

During the days which followed Jeremy became accustomed to the hard routine of work at Cressdale Mill. Each morning at 4 a.m. Old Gault stood at the foot of the stairs ringing a clamorous brass handbell to summon the apprentices to work. Five minutes were allowed for them to scramble from their bunks and since most of them went to sleep in their working clothes, dressing presented no difficulty, though a few of the more fortunate ones had clogs or hats to find in the dark dormitory. Everyone made haste to be out of the room before Old Gault arrived with his hazel stick to beat the laggards.

Jeremy found these dark winter mornings the hardest time to bear. There was no heating in the Apprentice House and the cold penetrated to the marrow. He was even glad that there was no time to wash, for washing on such black frosty mornings would have been unendurable. And yet, all around him, he had ample evidence of the effects of neglect and dirt. Boys and girls with infested hair and running sores—he had no intention of becoming like them. He took care to wash each night after work, though sometimes he was so tired that only his iron self-discipline kept him to it.

Straight from their bunks the children were marched across the rime-coated cobbles of the yard to the mill where the slow clanking of the paddle wheel told them that another day's work was commencing.

Once inside the mill, the apprentices dispersed to their various tasks where they were superintended by journey-man spinners and overseers like Jem Marsh. Some, usually the youngest, were put on piecing, that is, mending breaks in the swiftly running threads; others were kept busy doffing or removing the finished product at each stage of processing, whilst the remainder were occupied with winding rovings, carding, and the multiplicity of other jobs to be found in a busy cotton mill.

The mill smelt of oil and grease. Tiny wisps of cotton floated in the air like lost snowflakes, settling on clothes and hair and sticking to the oil of the machinery. The frantic click-clacking of the mules as they spun round and shot back and forth was quite incredible, like a million men with little hammers, and in the background, as a constant reminder of the power that drove it all, was the dull booming thresh of the mill wheel.

Though he was kept busy enough at his own job on the

hoist, there were occasions when Jeremy was sent errands
to other parts of the mill by Jem Marsh, and in this way
he came to know more about the mysterious machinery
and how it converted the fluffy cotton wool into a fine
strong thread.

He discovered that there were three main processes:
carding, drafting and spinning, before the yarn was
finished. The bales of raw cotton were broken open and
passed to the scutchers which turned it into a soft downy
sheet called lap. Then came the carding, the one he liked
the least. The soft lap was combed by toothed rollers into
a gossamer like sheet which in turn was rolled into long,
soft ropes called slivers. During the process all the cotton
staples which were broken or were too short to be spun
were removed, and it was the finer bits which escaped
and filled the mill with the choking white filaments.

From the carding machine the slivers were passed
through a draw frame, four at a time, and drawn together
until they were completely intermingled and stretched
to the thickness of a single sliver. This had the effect of
pulling the long cotton fibres parallel, ready for the real
stretching on the drafting frames.

As far as Jeremy could make out, the drafting was done
in four stages, each of which drafted the sliver six times—
that is, stretched it by rollers to six times its original
length. At each stage the yarn, now called rovings, was
twisted to give it strength and wound on to bobbins. From
time to time a roving would snap and it was an apprentice's job hurriedly to piece it up again, but in the main
the children were kept busy doffing the bobbins as they
became full.

The actual spinning frames—the final process—
occupied the best part of two floors and Jeremy watched

fascinatedly as the rovings were pulled and twisted at incredible speed by the mules into fine strong thread.

'Aye, 'tis a gradely invention reet enough,' said a friendly overseer one day, as Jeremy watched. 'Dost tha know why it's cawd a *mule*? Because it's a cross between Hargreaves' spinning jenny and Arkwright's water frame: it's nayther one nor t'other, same as a mule is nayther donkey nor horse, but a bit o' both!'

'But why is it better than the jenny or the water frame?' Jeremy asked.

'Because it maks a stronger thread. Tha con ask ony weaver an' he'll tell thi plain—a yarn fro' a jenny is aw reet for a weft, but noan strong enough for a warp—and it's t'warp as bears t'strain i' cloth. But yarn fro' a mule— strong enough for owt!'

'The inventor must have been very clever,' said Jeremy, full of admiration.

'Sam Crompton? Oh, aye! He made it aw by hiself in his lodgin's in Bowton—that's in Lancashire, tha knows— an' he paid for it by playin' a fiddle in a theatre o' neets! 'Tis a pity he wern't as clever wi' money: Sam has no head for business and sharp folk like Mester Bradwell soon diddled him out o' his dues!'

These visits to other parts of the mill were something by way of treats for Jeremy—usually he was hard at work lifting and breaking bales, choking on the fluff from the carding machines.

At eight o'clock Old Gault brought round the apprentices' breakfast of thin water porridge, known locally as 'stir pudding', and stale oat cakes. There was no question of work stopping whilst this meal was eaten; work and eating went on simultaneously; the mules spun relentlessly.

At one o'clock, however, the booming of the water wheel suddenly stopped, and, cut off from their source of power, the machines rattled to a halt. The quick silence was disconcerting; it was as if the mill had suddenly died. On the first day when it happened Jeremy thought that there had been some mechanical breakdown, but no such luck—it was dinner time; forty minutes in which the apprentices had to trail to their lodging and eat whatever was left over from the supper of the previous evening.

Jeremy was fortunate in so far as he had the whole forty minutes free from work, but he soon found that most of the other apprentices were not so lucky. Twenty minutes were devoted to cleaning down the machines and oiling them, so that dinner time was halved. Sometimes the cleaning down took the entire forty minutes, in which case 'overtime' pay of one farthing was allowed, though it meant that anyone on overtime missed their dinner and went for twelve hours or more without a meal.

Little wonder that at the end of the day—eight or nine o'clock—the apprentices were thoroughly tired out. Sometimes the older boys would help the seven-year-olds back to the Apprentice House because the little ones were literally too tired to stand.

Hard work such as this was in itself enough to destroy the health and spirit of most youngsters, but added to it, piling torment on torture, was the unmerciful cruelty of the overseers. Marsh was by no means alone in his treatment of the apprentices, for though he had a reputation for brutality second to none, many of the others were equally cruel. Beatings, known locally as 'beltings' or 'flankings', were such an everyday feature of life at Cressdale that they passed unremarked. Nor was it uncommon for wooden rollers from the draw frames to be hurled at the heads of the unfortunate apprentices. Some overseers indulged in greater cruelties too, such as filing the children's teeth with rasps.

Almost anything an apprentice did could be held against him as a 'crime' and he was savagely punished or fined, or more often than not, both. Worst crime of all was to be slow or slipshod over the work itself and the punishment for this was to have a large iron weight tied on each wrist so that every movement was ten times more laborious. Thus encumbered the poor apprentice had to keep up with the rapid machines or suffer further punishment.

Though conditions at Cressdale were almost beyond endurance, Jeremy was amazed to discover that they were not exceptional and that there were others even worse. He learned this from apprentices who had been transferred from one master to another—a practice which was common, though illegal. Some of the tales they told made him shudder, especially when he learned that at some mills children who had tried to escape were shackled with leg irons for the rest of their apprenticeship.

Friday night at Cressdale Mill was bath night; the one occasion during the week when the youngsters tried to remove all the grease and dirt from their bodies. The washing took place in the dining hall and was absolute pandemonium. Whilst the older boys were kept busy fetching water from the well behind the Apprentice House, the girls were put in charge of scrubbing the younger urchins, all of whom objected strongly at the tops of their voices. Shouts and screams mingled with terrible curses and the violent splashing of water. For soap, which Bradwell reckoned was too dear for pauper children to waste, they were given a handful of oatmeal, but this proved such a poor substitute that most of the apprentices ate it instead and preferred to take their luck at getting clean by plain cold water. Not surprisingly, despite all the noise and action, bath night seldom achieved its purpose.

On one such a Friday night, Jeremy, who through regular washing had no need for such drastic action, was watching the scene with some amusement when he felt a tug at his sleeve. Turning, he found Moses Gault at his elbow.

'Come along 'o me, young un,' wheezed the apprentice master. 'Ah've getten a job for thee.'

Jeremy followed Old Gault into the latter's kitchen which seemed strangely quiet after the babel of the apprentices' room.

In the kitchen, which was warm and smelt of cooking, he found Mrs Gault with a stranger he had not seen before, and a young apprentice from the carding called Billy Barlow. The stranger was a well dressed man, with grey hair and spectacles. He was stirring the contents of a small iron pot which balanced precariously on the glowing coals of the fire. Young Billy was watching him in horrified fascination.

'We've brung Doctor Green fro' Chapel to hev a look at young Billy here,' said Gault by way of explanation. 'Billy's getten a sore yead—hasn't tha, Billy?'

' 'Sright enough, Mr Gault—but I ain't certain I likes what the doctor's a-doin' for it,' said the apprentice apprehensively. He scratched his head nervously.

'What's wrong with your head, Billy?' Jeremy asked.

'It itches.'

'Lice,' said Doctor Green, in a thin piping voice. 'Lice and sores. If it ain't treated he'll get blood poisoning and die. A good pitch poultice is what he needs!'

'But how can I be of service?' Jeremy asked, in a puzzled tone.

'To hold him down, o' course!' Doctor Green replied, in a voice which indicated he thought the question unnecessary. Billy began to cry.

'Stop thi' skrikin'—ungrateful brat!' commanded Gault. 'Nah then, Jeremy, grab howd on him!'

The advice came just in time, for Billy, frightened of what might happen, tried to make a dash for the door. Gault and Jeremy seized him and held him down in a chair, whilst the doctor, apparently satisfied with the hotness of the pot, ladled from it a large spoonful of sticky black pitch. Without more ado he poured it over the boy's scalp ignoring completely the cries of pain from his unfortunate patient.

In a moment or two the pitch cooled and set like a shiny black cap on the boy's head. Doctor Green stood behind him and reaching over, gripped the front of the pitch cap where it met Billy's forehead. 'Hold him tight now!' he ordered—and with a quick jerk of his wrist he ripped off the pitch like a grocer stripping cloth from a cheese.

Billy gave a scream which made Mrs Gault drop the pan she was holding and almost caused Jeremy to let go his grip. Then he subsided into low moans, and Jeremy could see that the pitch cap had completely scalped him! In place of his hair there was a bald pate as clean and pink as the skin of a newly born babe!

'Ah!' said Doctor Green, with evident satisfaction at a job well done. 'I think that will do very nicely!'

When Jeremy left the Gaults' kitchen he was more determined than ever that he would keep himself clean and fit. He had no desire to undergo the drastic treatment of the pitch cap himself!

He made his way upstairs to his bunk. Waiting for him he found Little Joey, less than his usual cheery self. 'What's the matter, Joey?' Jeremy asked. 'You look a might soulful this evening.'

'It ain't good news I bears, mate, an' that's a fact.'

'What do you mean?'

'The Devil himself comes back tomorrer.'

Jeremy gave him a look of incomprehension.

'Harrison Bradwell!'

CHAPTER SIX

HARRISON BRADWELL

SO MUCH HAD happened since his arrival at Cressdale that Jeremy had entirely forgotten the very existence of Harrison Bradwell. It seemed that the mill-owner's son had been absent on business in Manchester, and more pressing affairs had driven all thought of him from Jeremy's mind.

But the mention of his name was sufficient to bring flooding back memories of Bradwell's savage assault in Chapel en le Frith. For some reason which was quite beyond Jeremy's comprehension, Harrison hated him, and the apprentice realised that the humiliating punishment Bradwell had received from Mendoza would not be forgotten or forgiven.

When he told Joey his story, the little Londoner was appalled. He gave his candid opinion that Jeremy was a doomed man. 'He never forgets, mate,' he said bitterly. 'Not ever. For Gawd's sake keep low and say nuffink.'

It certainly seemed to be sound advice for it was at once apparent throughout the entire mill that Harrison had returned in a foul temper. He had had a furious row with his father—though nobody knew why—and he cursed everything and everyone he came across. Even the overseers came in for their share, and they in turn took it out on the apprentices.

Jem Marsh was one of the first to suffer. He came back to the loft in a quivering rage.

' 'Tis a damned good job he's t'mester's son,' he cried savagely to his awe-struck apprentices. 'Or ah'd hev kilt him. So help me, than an' I would!' His eye fell on Jeremy, and something seemed to jog his memory. 'An' thee watch out, Mester Jeremy! Ah've geet a notion theer's some sort o' feud a-tween thee and t'Bradwells, but mark my words—Harrison is noan to be takken lightly! Watch thi step—or he'll hev thi hide!'

Fortunately Jeremy did not meet Harrison that day and as time wore on he began to feel more confident.

On the following morning he had scarcely finished his stir pudding when he heard the voice of Joshua Bradwell calling him from the mill-yard. Jem Marsh heard it too. 'Tha wanted,' he said. 'Hurry thisel—mester doan't like waitin'.'

By this time Jeremy had fallen in with the common practice of sliding down the hoist rope to the yard. Every time he did it it reminded him of that first meeting with Marsh, but at least it saved him having to run down all those steps! In less than a minute he was in the yard, facing the mill-owner.

Bradwell was not a man to beat about the bush. He came to the point immediately and abruptly. 'Con tha read and write?' he demanded.

'Yes,' replied Jeremy, who persistently refused to address Bradwell as 'sir' or 'master'.

Surprisingly, he received no clout round the ear for disrespect. The mill-owner seemed too preoccupied to notice the insult. He asked, 'An' con tha do figures—arithmetic and such like?'

Jeremy nodded, wondering what it was all about.

Bradwell seemed to be pondering on his replies and trying to make up his mind about something. At last he said, half to himself, 'Ah've never been much a one for figurin' meself—but I reckoned a lad like thee might have some learnin'.' He shot Jeremy a keen glance, then, as if making up his mind, said, 'Ah've getten a job for thee. Coom wi' me.'

He turned swiftly on his heels and led the way across the cobbled yard to a single storeyed building adjoining the mill which Jeremy knew to be the Counting House. Though he had never been inside it, he had heard that it was the office where everything that entered the mill in the way of stores was accounted for, and likewise the finished thread.

Bradwell thrust open the door and they went inside. It was spacious and clean, with plastered walls and a bright fire burning in a grate at one end; a startling contrast with the mill it served. Shelves lined the walls, all piled with ledgers and papers, and at the far end, by a bright window, was a high mahogony counting desk and stool. Only a quill pen, an inkpot and a sand blotter furnished the desk, but on a small side table there were papers, old bills and folded letters stamped with the fascinating Bishop marks which showed their place of origin. It was the first office that Jeremy had ever seen and he wondered what one could do with so much paper.

'Sit thisel' down,' ordered Bradwell, brusquely, pointing to the stool.

Jeremy did as he was bid and the mill owner pulled a heavy calf-bound ledger from a shelf and thumped it on the desk in front of him.

'These are some of t'accounts for t'last twelve month,' he explained. 'But ah'm noan satisfied wi' 'em. Ah wants thee to add 'em up an' see if they're reet. If they're not— then tha mon let me know at once.' He gripped Jeremy violently by the arm so that the boy let out a yelp of pain. 'And mark, thee,' he added fiercely, 'tha' speaks on this to no one.' He turned quickly and left the room.

Jeremy was dazed at the mill owner's odd behaviour. As he took up a penknife and sharpened the quill he tried to think what reasons lay behind Bradwell's request. One thing was for sure—the man himself was uneducated and unable to check his own accounts. Moreover, it looked as though whoever did keep the accounts was not entirely trusted.

The reason for this quickly became apparent once Jeremy started to check the figures in the ledger. They simply did not add up correctly. At first he thought he had made some mistake, but when he tried again with the same result he began to delve more deeply into the individual entries. It had been cleverly done—a slight alteration here and there, sufficient to deceive anyone giving the book a casual glance—but as month followed month in the ledger it became quite clear that someone was systematically swindling the mill of hundreds of pounds!

Jeremy scarcely knew whether to be shocked or pleased at his discovery: shocked because of the enormity of the crime, or pleased because it was his hated enemy who was being swindled. He sat, chin in hands, wondering whether to tell Bradwell the bad news, or whether to let him go on being robbed.

Suddenly the door opened and Harrison Bradwell entered the room. On seeing Jeremy perched on the stool he stopped in sheer surprise. Then his eye fell on the open ledger and his face went dark with anger.

'What the Deuce—!' he cried, springing forward and grabbing the ledger. Thumping it shut, he flung it on to a shelf and turned on Jeremy. Seizing him by the shoulders he shook him as a dog might shake a rabbit.

'Spy on me, would ye?' he cried, white with rage. 'I'll teach ye to spy ye demmed rascal!'

He flung Jeremy from the high stool on to the floor with a crash which shook the room, then, spinning round, he reached for a long horse-whip which was hanging neatly coiled behind the door. He was quite mad with rage and there was no doubt that he intended to flay Jeremy alive.

Trapped between Bradwell and the wall, Jeremy thought rapidly. Though he knew Harrison hated him and wanted to get even for the thrashing he had received from Mendoza, that hardly accounted for such a sudden outburst. And what did Harrison mean by *spying*? The truth hit him like a sledge-hammer—*it was Harrison who kept the accounts book and it was Harrison who was swindling his own father!*

The irony of it almost made Jeremy laugh, but Harrison Bradwell, armed with a whip, was no laughing matter. As Bradwell raised the whip to strike, Jeremy cried sharply, 'Hold!'

Taken aback, Bradwell let the whip fall to his side.

'Touch me, Harrison Bradwell,' Jeremy cried, 'and I'll see you swing in Derby Jail!'

Bradwell hesitated and Jeremy added, quickly, 'I've read the accounts—on your father's orders.'

Harrison blanched. A look of wild fear leapt into his eyes as he realised the fraud had been uncovered. Nevertheless he tried to bluster it out.

'Those accounts are special,' he lied. 'They do not show everything.'

'They show enough to hang a man for embezzlement!'

Despite his appearance of refinement; his dandy clothes and his education at Rugby School, Harrison Bradwell was a stupid man. Faced with an unalterable truth he tried to counter it by piling lie upon lie, hoping to convince Jeremy that there was nothing wrong with the accounts— and all the time condemning himself out of his own mouth.

'My father knows all about the slight discrepancies,' he said hotly. 'They are nothing unusual.'

'Then you will not mind me telling him about them,' Jeremy replied. 'Though 'tis strange he should ask.'

'Ah, yes—well the fact is that things are not up to date. I've been away in Manchester. But the money will be returned quite soon. Every penny piece.' A sweat had appeared on his forehead.

'Your father will be glad to hear it,' replied Jeremy coldly.

'No! 'Twere best he did not hear on't. If he asks, I beg you say nothing. He's an uneducated man—he has not the learning that you and I possess—and he might not understand.'

Jeremy remained silent, nauseated at Harrison's manner. The latter babbled on. ' 'Tis all one to you, aint it? Say nothing to my father and I'll be obleeged. Look—I will make your stay at the mill more comfortable—put you on lighter tasks.'

Jeremy nodded. 'So be it,' he said curtly as if in agreement. 'And now I'll be about my business.'

He walked out into the yard feeling as though he had just missed death by a hair's breadth. What a despicable person Harrison Bradwell was, and yet how just that Joshua should have such a son! All the same, he knew that the matter could not rest there and a cold finger of fear touched his spine as he realised what a dangerous situation he was in. With the evidence he possessed Harrison Bradwell could be hung and Harrison was not the sort of person to live under continual threat. Harrison would try to kill him, that much was certain.

When Jeremy left the Counting House, Harrison Bradwell gave vent to a fit of wild rage. He hammered his fists impotently on the desk and kicked the stool to the far side of the room.

Damn Ollershaw for an interfering little brat! The boy would talk and that would ruin everything—but what could be done about it? Destroy the evidence? Hardly. His father was suspicious already and if the ledger was destroyed his suspicions would be confirmed. Joshua Bradwell might be illiterate, but he was not a fool. The trouble was, there was no chance of repaying the money—gambling debts incurred by gaming with his rich city friends had seen to that.

Ollershaw was the dangerous link—he could see that quite clearly. With a bit of luck he might be able to fool his father over the books, or at least gain some time, but if the apprentice blabbed, everything would be lost.

A hard look came over Harrison Bradwell's face as he realised that Jeremy Ollershaw would have to die. In a mill like Cressdale accidents were a commonplace and the Coroner never enquired too closely into the cause of death—after all, what was one pauper more or less? If an 'accident' could be arranged for Ollershaw, it might solve a lot of things . . .

But Bradwell shrank at the thought of performing the deed himself. He seldom went into the mill—it was far too noisy and dirty for a gentleman as refined as he—so it would be difficult for him to get at the boy. His very presence would arouse suspicion. Besides which, though Ollershaw might technically die of an accident, Harrison knew that what he really contemplated was murder.

He sat on the stool and thought deeply. He would have to acquire an accomplice—one not too particular about the lives of apprentices, but with a certain natural cunning. There was only one man he knew who fitted perfectly—Jem Marsh.

'Tha sent for me, Mester Harrison?' Jem Marsh demanded, when he appeared in the Counting House in response to a message from Bradwell.

'That I did, Jem—I'm obleeged to thee for coming so promptly.'

Marsh's eyes narrowed for a moment with a flicker of suspicion. This was a very different Harrison Bradwell from the man who had cursed him so roundly only the previous day. He said nothing, waiting to see what it was that Bradwell wanted.

'You and I have had our differences in the past, Jem,' Harrison began smoothly, smiling at the overseer, 'but by mi' faith, I do think the error was on my side. You have sterling qualities, Jem—qualities which go altogether unrecognized.' He shook his head as though the thought saddened him. 'Were I master here, you would have preferment.'

Marsh let the empty words wash over him, saying nothing in reply.

'Of course the day will come when my father passes over Jordan, and I shall inherit Cressdale Mill. I shall not forget those who have served me well, when that day comes.'

Marsh was a plain spoken man and Harrison's silver tongue grated on his nature. Unable to contain himself he said brusquely, 'Aw reet, Mester Harrison, Ah taks thi' meaning. What is it tha wants?'

Bradwell chose his words carefully, looking the overseer straight in the eye. 'First I want your word that whatever passes between us in this room shall go no further.'

Marsh nodded.

'Good. What do you know about a 'prentice who calls himself Jeremy Ollershaw?'

'Nowt—except that he works under me.'

'Excellent! Suppose young Master Ollershaw were to meet with an accident?'

'That's noan likely—he's too sharp.'

Harrison smiled grimly. 'Come now, Jem!' he said. 'You know that accidents can happen to even the best 'prentice. A moment's carelessness by the hoist door and *poof!*— Master Ollershaw has fallen thirty feet to the mill yard, poor lad. Very sad, no doubt, but such things happen. Do you not agree?'

Marsh's face was a study in granite. Only his eyes glittered. He was silent for a moment, then he said. 'I wants no part on it. A flankin's one thing, but murder is a hangin' matter.'

Harrison held up his hands in mock horror. 'Who spoke of murder?' he demanded. 'I was talking of accidents— no Coroner ever questioned an accident.'

'Caw it how tha likes,' Marsh retorted angrily. 'But I caws it murder.'

'Are you growing soft in your old age, Marsh?' Harrison demanded in a hard voice, all pretence gone. 'There's money in this.'

'Ah'm noan soft—but ah'm noan soft in t'head nayther. Ah've knowed all along as how theer was summat goo-in on between yo Bradwells and young Ollershaw—summat a mite queer, by my reckonin'—an' ah wants no part on it. Yon lad is no' an ordinary 'prentice, wi' aw his fine talk an'

4

brown skin. Tha's only getten for t'look at his face to know he's from t'gentry, an' if he dees there'll be Hell to pay! Why! For aw I knows he met be a Cavendish or a Bagshawe—an' tha couldn't hide *that* at no inquest. Oh, no, Mester Harrison—ah'm havin' nowt to do wi' young Ollershaw. Tha mun do thi own dirty work!'

And Jem Marsh stamped out of the Counting House, leaving Harrison Bradwell perplexed and angry.

After dinner, which he took at noon in the Factor's House, Harrison was even more angry. His father had scarcely spoken a civil word to him and for a while he suspected that Jeremy had already given the game away. The bright winter sunshine, which made the trees glitter and put hopes of spring in most men's hearts, went unnoticed by him. Everything was going wrong, and like the stupid man he was, he felt like striking out blindly at everything and everybody, to vent his rage.

He went out into the mill-yard looking for victims. First he cursed Frederick Small, a little wizened overseer from the spinning department, for no reason at all, then he boxed the ears of two girl apprentices for giggling on their way back to work after dinner. Others who saw these things happen, made haste to get out of his way. It was not wise to cross Master Harrison when he was in one of his moods.

Harrison strolled across the yard in the direction of the river: the pounding of the great mill wheel felt like an echo to the pounding of his own brain and drew him like a magnet. When he came to the mill race he paused to watch the water go rushing along like a mountain torrent. The force came from damming the river about a hundred yards upstream from the mill, and by means of a specially constructed channel, about four feet deep and six wide, carrying the rushing water to the overshot wheel. This was the 'race', and because it stole most of the water from the river, the bed of the main stream was rocky and shallow until the race waters returned to it after turning the wheel.

A small footbridge crossed the race, giving access to the river. Harrison stood on this eyeing the stream and the mill with baleful looks. Suddenly his attention was caught by a small boy fishing in the shallow river. Harrison recognized him at once as Joey Walls, the crippled apprentice.

All the pent up rage within Bradwell was directed at poor Joey. What right had an apprentice to enjoy himself fishing in the river, even in his dinner hour?

'Walls!' he cried, 'Come up here, you demmed rascal!'

Joey had not seen Bradwell and he was so startled by this sudden summons that he dropped his home-made rod into the stream. Nevertheless, he did not dare stop to retrieve it for he could see that Harrison was in a temper. As quickly as he was able he hobbled up the steep river bank towards the footbridge.

'Caught ye skulking, ain't I?' cried Bradwell, dealing him a vicious blow round the head.

'I'm only fishin', Mester Harrison,' Joey whimpered, afraid of the big man. ' 'Tis my dinner time. I wern't doin' no harm, honest!'

Since Harrison had roared at the top of his voice, th commotion had attracted a considerable crowd of idlers Overseers and apprentices stared up from the yard towards the race embankment to see what all the row was about, and since word had got round that Harrison was in a bad temper there was a feeling of sympathy for Joey.

'Let the lad be!' somebody shouted. A murmer of assent

came from the crowd. Harrison turned to face them, livid with rage.

'Who said that?' he screamed. 'What scurvy mongrel dares to talk to me in such a fashion?'

The crowd remained silent. Harrison treated them to a contemptuous sneer. 'Cowards, the lot of ye! I'll show thee who's master in this mill!' His eyes were unnaturally bright and flecks of froth ran down from the corners of his mouth. To the watchers it seemed that he had gone beyond normal anger; that he was demented to the point of frenzy.

'So ye like river banks, do ye, Walls?' he demanded savagely, turning on Joey again. 'Then here's a bonny bank. Walk the mill race to its furthest end!'

A gasp of horror went up from the crowd as they heard this. The parapet of the mill race was just one stone block in width. On its outside it dropped twenty feet in a steep embankment to the mill yard whilst on the inside the waters roared along the channel to the mill wheel.

An active youngster with agility and a steady head might have done it, but for a cripple like Joey it was suicidal.

'I can't walk the coping, Mister Harrison,' whined the apprentice, tearfully. 'I'll fall in and be drowned!'

But Harrison Bradwell was beyond reason. 'Walk it, dem you, or I'll throw ye in!' he shouted.

He grabbed Joey and shoved him along the parapet. The boy staggered, found his balance, and stood shivering on the narrow ledge.

A grey haired man detached himself from the crowd and made for the footbridge. It was Ben Wilson, the elderly mill carpenter who was liked by everyone for his kindly disposition. Now he was angry, intent on stopping Harrison's madness.

'Let t'lad alone!' he commanded. 'Cawn't tha see he's a cripple?'

Bradwell hit the carpenter square on the chin, sending him sprawling down the embankment into the arms of the crowd.

'Now start walking!' he shrieked at Joey.

The crowd watched with sullen anger as the little cripple edged along the parapet. Inch by inch he limped his way along the narrow copings and the crowd became deathly silent. Only the dull booming of the mill wheel played a solemn background music to Joey's tight-rope.

Whether it was the silence of the crowd, or the throbbing of the mill wheel, or whether all his rage was spent Harrison Bradwell suddenly came to his senses. Something snapped, leaving him cold, and the enormity of what he was doing to the little cripple swept over him like a wave.

'All right! That's far enough—come back,' he cried, an edge of fear tainting his voice.

Overjoyed at his sudden and unexpected reprieve, Little Joey tried to turn round. For a moment his concentration relaxed, and for a split second he was off balance. Wildly he flung out his arms to prevent himself from falling and he rocked dangerously from one foot to the other. For a moment he seemed to be all right, but his crippled foot was no proper support. His leg gave way and with a terrible shriek he plunged into the mill race.

There was no hope of saving him. The water roared along the race carrying the helpless boy with it. At the end, beyond a dark tunnel, the mill wheel churned relentlessly.

For a moment the crowd was too stunned to move. Then a mass anger welled up to burst like a bomb. With a savage roar they rushed towards the footbridge intent on pitching Bradwell into the race after his victim.

But Harrison was too quick for them. He made a desperate leap down the embankment, stumbled, scrambled to his feet and ran for the safety of the mill.

Like a pack of hounds after their quarry the mob ran after him. They tore through the mill like a tornado, and rumour ran with them, wild, hysterical rumour fanning the latent flames of hatred for the Bradwells and Cressdale Mill. Years of injustice and cruelty which the apprentices had suffered suddenly swelled and burst into a desire for revenge.

Within minutes the mob was completely out of hand. Had either of the Bradwells been present they would have been torn limb from limb, but as it was, it was the mill which suffered instead. Machines were smashed, bobbins were thrown through the windows and whole bales of cotton were hurled into the yard until the place seemed like a battlefield. From the mill itself they rampaged through the storehouse and even the Apprentice House, where Old Gault and his wife, fearing for their lives, locked themselves in their kitchen, trembling.

For an hour the mob ran riot, breaking and destroying everything they could lay hands on. But they did not find Harrison Bradwell.

It ended as suddenly as it had begun. A twelve-year-old girl apprentice, Molly Kirk, intent on smashing the windows of the Apprentice House suddenly let out a scream which could be heard even above the uproar of the mob.

'T'mill's afire!' she shouted.

Wisps of smoke were curling out of the lower windows of Cressdale Mill and a dull red glow could be seen spreading through the ground floor. Ten minutes later the mill was a blazing inferno.

CHAPTER SEVEN

THE CAVE

FROM HIS PLACE by the mill hoist, Jeremy had been a helpless witness to the death of Little Joey. The shock of it numbed him. The little Londoner had been his staunchest friend at the mill, and there had been times when his Cockney cheerfulness had saved Jeremy from despair. He could hardly believe that Joey was dead; that anyone could be so senselessly cruel.

When the crowd surged after Harrison Bradwell, Jeremy had raced to the footbridge to gaze at the swirling waters of the mill race, as though he might still find his lost friend, though he knew in his heart that it was quite hopeless for anyone to survive such a maelstrom.

Nevertheless, he scrambled down the bank to the river in the faint hope that Joey had been carried straight through by the rush of water, had somehow missed the mangling blades of the wheel, and been cast up on the far side by the outflow channel.

For half an hour Jeremy searched the outflow channel, even the river itself, but there was no sign of Joey. Once or twice his hopes soared as he thought he saw a figure caught in the rushes, but always it turned out to be nothing but driftwood; the flotsam of a working river.

It was never more than the faintest of hopes and bit by bit even this evaporated. Jeremy collapsed in grief on the river's bank, and putting his head in his arms, sobbed.

How long he stayed there he could not tell. Lost in

his sorrow at the death of Joey the commotion at the mill went by unheeded. It was the sight of Harrison Bradwell which brought him to his senses.

Bradwell appeared on the river bank as if from nowhere, wild eyed and dishevelled. His jacket was gone and his white, lace-frilled shirt was torn and stained with oil, his pale blue breeches sullied with mud.

Jeremy quickly rolled under a bush out of sight, but it was obvious that Harrison had not seen him. He was too intent on his own business. In his hands he carried a small bundle of oily waste, such as was used to clean the machinery. Under the cover of the tall mill walls he proceeded to light this from his pocket tinder box, and soon he was holding a smouldering torch. Taking deliberate aim, he hurled the smoking bundle through the mob-shattered windows of the Counting House.

Jeremy watched this performance with amazement, convinced that Harrison Bradwell had finaily gone out of his mind altogether, but then he realised what was happening. The villain was using the riot at the mill as a cover for an attempt to save his own neck. If the mill burnt, then the ledgers containing the accounts would be destroyed, and he would be freed from suspicion.

As soon as Harrison had gone, Jeremy sprang to his feet and raced towards the burning Counting House. There was no time to run round into the mill yard in order to enter the building by its door, for already great volumes of smoke were pouring from the window. Jeremy scrambled up the rocky bank and tackled the rough stone walls of the building until he could grasp the window sill and pull himself in.

He landed in a heap, coughing and spluttering as the dense smoke caught at his throat. Already the far end where the rags had landed was fairly ablaze and he could feel sudden, searing gusts of heat as the flames billowed and lapped at the paper-filled room.

Fortunately he could remember exactly where Harrison had flung the ledger that morning. Seizing it, he threw it out of the window and quickly dropped out after it.

For a few moments he lay on the ground by the gently gurgling river, recovering his breath. He felt like retching from the effects of the smoke, but this passed and it was only then that he realised his hands and arms were nicked in a dozen places from the raw glass edges of the window.

No matter. The important thing was that he had saved the mill accounts. With the evidence in the ledger he was determined to avenge the death of Little Joey.

Picking up the heavy volume and tucking it under his arm, Jeremy made his way along the strip of land between the mill and the river until he came to open fields. He had to get away—that much was certain. He had to reach Nook Hall as quickly as possible, and trust that Sam Ollershaw would be able to help him.

He cut across the fields to the Cressdale road and plunged once again into the familiar woods. Behind him the mill burnt fiercely.

By the middle of the afternoon Cressdale Mill was nothing more than a smoke-blackened shell. The effect of the fire had been to stun the rioters into common-sense: they had turned from their destructive rampage and set up a human chain to handle buckets of water from the mill race to the fire, in vain a attempt to save the building. But the fire had too good a hold and by midday the workers knew they had lost the struggle. One by one the floors had collapsed with thunderous roars and leaping

4*

flames, until finally the roof caved in and the fire smouldered to extinction.

When it was all over everyone gathered in the mill yard to face a grey countenanced, embittered Joshua Bradwell. The mill owner's clothes were torn and stained from fire-fighting, and he was almost dropping from fatigue, but his eyes glittered venomously. Though he had cannily insured the mill against such damage at Lloyd's Coffee House in London, when he first went into business, nevertheless he felt bitter about seeing his life's work reduced to smouldering ashes.

'I hopes that each an' every one o' yo' is satisfied wi' this day's work! he cried bitterly. 'T'mill is gone and wi' it is gone thy bread an' butter!'

' 'Twere noan us as fired t'mill,' shouted one of the older apprentices.

'No? Then who were it, pray? Find him an' by God I'll hev him strung up at t'next Derby Assize!'

Harrison was standing by his father's side, confident that nobody had seen him fire the mill. Indeed he had played a heroic part in fighting the blaze, though he was well satisfied when he saw the Counting House collapse in flames. It had gone even better than he dared hope: the accounts were destroyed and the fire itself had made everyone forget the death of Little Joey.

Smugly he looked around to see where Jeremy was and when he failed to find him among the other apprentices, he realised the boy must have run away again. Here was a splendid opportunity for revenge!

'Where's Jeremy Ollershaw?' he cried to the crowd.

A buzz went up as everyone turned round to see who was their neighbour. 'He's noan here,' someone cried. 'Happen he's run off agin!'

Joshua Bradwell was out of patience. 'Damn Ollershaw,' he shouted. 'Theer's moor to think on than him, now!'

'But it could have been him who fired the mill,' Harrison slyly suggested.

'Happen that's why he's run off,' Jem Marsh shouted from the edge of the crowd. 'He were allus a deep 'un, young Ollershaw. 'Twould be just like him to fire t'mill and run off while everyone were occupied wi' fire-feighting!'

Joshua Bradwell seized on the idea at once. Here was a glorious opportunity for catching a culprit and at the same time putting paid to Ollershaw once and for all. Not for an instant did he believe in Marsh's theory that Jeremy had deliberately set fire to the mill—he secretly thought it was an accident caused through the rioting—but the need for a scapegoat was real, and Joshua had his own reasons for wanting Jeremy out of the way.

'Aye!' he cried aloud. 'He were allus a rebel, yon mon. But he'll noan escape! I'll swear a warrant for his arrest!'

'A warrant takes too long,' said Harrison. 'Let's catch him first—he can't have gotten far. Five guineas to the man that catches Jeremy Ollershaw!'

The crowd gave a whoop of delight. Tired though they were with fighting the fire the thought of a five guinea prize gave them new energy. Like packs of hounds they split into small bands and went rushing out of the yard with yells and cries.

Harrison turned to his father with a grim smile of satisfaction. 'Fools!' he said. 'They'll run o'er half the country and not find him. Ollershaw's too clever for a rabble like that.'

'Aye. He's sharp enough to outwit 'em,' agreed his father. 'But he's geet for t'mak his way to Nook Hall, an' like as not he'll tak t'Castleton road.'

'Then let us take a similar path on our horses,' said Harrison, grimly. 'And we'll settle young master Ollershaw once and for all!'

At first Jeremy had plunged through the woods oblivious of all sense of direction. It was only when he sank exhausted in a sheltered glade that he decided he had better make proper plans for reaching Nook Hall.

He recognized his surroundings from his previous escape. He was in the narrow wooded dale flanked by the high limestone cliffs which he had followed once before. He knew that if he went off to his right he would fetch up in the village of Wardlow, where he was captured, and he had no intention of risking the same fate again. Instead, he decided to follow the dale to its end and see where it led him.

It was much easier to make his way through the woods in daylight than it was during his night-time adventures of his previous escape. A narrow path twisted through the trees and before long came out into the upper part of the dale which was a narrow grassy defile containing nothing but a clear running stream. On either hand the banks of the dale rose steeply, cutting off any view of the surrounding countryside, and Jeremy felt like a blind man, trapped in a green alley.

Then he had his first piece of luck. On the right of the dale there arose a curious pinnacle of limestone, like a watch tower, from which he could spy out the land. He clambered up the steep but easy rocks to a knife-edged summit and looked out on a world of bright green limestone fields, such as Sam Ollershaw had once described to him. Near at hand he could see a road, and he was sure it was the same road that had once brought him to Cressdale Mill from Nook Hall, and away in the distance he thought he could spy the high dark hills of Kynder Scwd.

It took him but five minutes to reach the highway and he set off manfully in the direction of Nook Hall. Though he could now go fairly quickly, Jeremy felt curiously unhappy about his exposed situation. The fact was that he had grown used to the shelter of the trees and the dale, whereas the open road seemed frighteningly without cover. And Jeremy knew, that sooner or later, cover would be essential.

He had walked for about a mile along the road, still splendidly hard from frost, when he came upon a fingerpost marking a parting of the ways. His heart leapt—this was the very place where he and the Justices' Clerk had turned off to go to Cressdale. Now he knew for certain that he was on the right road.

Still, he would have liked some cover, and as if in answer to his silent wishes, he heard a sudden clanking noise and saw that it came from a strange sort of covered cart which was approaching the cross-roads from Tideswell. It was pulled by a single, tired looking nag, and driven by a man who looked for all the world like a pirate.

Jeremy had never seen a gypsy before and he scarcely knew what to make of it all. The cart was brightly painted in reds and yellows, and the clanking came from dozens of pots and pans which hung festooned along its sides. Though it made slow progress it nevertheless soon drew level with Jeremy and he had an opportunity of observing the driver more closely.

The man was young—about twenty-five at a guess— with a dark swarthy skin and black hair which hung to his shoulders and was kept in place by a bright red kerchief. Gold rings hung from his ears, and he wore a white shirt with a coloured waistcoat, fancy breeks and long boots.

'Hello there, young friend,' the man called cheerfully as he drew abreast. 'That's a fine big book you are a-carrying though a mite heavy on the arms, I'd say.'

'It is indeed, sir,' Jeremy replied.

'Can I help you on your way? I'm bound for Chapel en le Frith, providing old Bess—that's the horse, you'll mind—feels up to the journey.'

Jeremy took an immediate liking to the gypsy. He knew instinctively that here was a man who wanted to help him and was not a traitor like the tailor at Wardlow. He liked especially the way in which the man did not enquire who he was, or what he was doing. He accepted the gypsy's offer and climbed up on to the seat beside him.

'They tell me that learning is a wonderful thing,' the gypsy remarked, as the old horse settled into its steady plod again. 'Though I am but a simple Romany who does not know such things.'

'Did you not go to school in your parish?' Jeremy asked innocently.

The gypsy laughed pleasantly, showing fine white teeth. 'This is my school,' he said, indicating the country-side. 'And all the world is my parish. I confess I cannot construe a single word of Latin, no, nor write my name, either—but I know the coverts where the partridge hide and I know which herbs will mend a broken bone. Now I ask you, young sir, which is the more useful knowledge?'

'Why, undoubtedly you have the advantage of me, sir,' replied Jeremy, 'but do not think that other kinds of learning are without their uses. This book I carry will bring a cruel man to justice.'

The gypsy glanced at the book with troubled eyes. 'Knowledge such as that can be dangerous,' he said briefly.

For half an hour the caravan rumbled on its way. The gypsy was full of interesting conversation. He told Jeremy how he earned his living as a tinker, which was why he carried so many pots and pans, and how he wandered all over England, as the fancy took him.

'The face of England is changing,' he said, with a trace of sadness in his voice. 'The common land and the open heath which belonged to the people is fast disappearing behind the squire's hedges.

'Clear streams where once a man might catch a fat trout are now blackened with slime from ugly mills. Some places are worse than others—you should observe the town of Birmingham, young sir. Eight hundred blast furnaces they do say, and a pall of sulphurous smoke which never clears even on the brightest day, and can be seen for miles around. Huge heaps of spoil which the natives call *slag* frown down on miserable hovels where men, women and children live like rabbits in a warren. 'Tis Hades itself! Little wonder men call it the *Black Country*.'

As the road began to wind down towards the small hamlet of Peak Forest, the gypsy suddenly stopped his discourse, and tilted his head on one side, as if listening to something which only he could hear.

'Horsemen—two I think—riding hard behind us,' he said.

'I hear nothing,' Jeremy said in a puzzled tone.

' 'Tis the clangour of the pots distracts your hearing,' the Romany explained. 'But I can hear them well enough.'

Clambering on to the seat in order to look back over the roof of the caravan, Jeremy could see two riders galloping like the wind from the direction of Tideswell. Though they were still some distance away, he had no difficulty in recognizing Joshua Bradwell and his son.

A wave of panic swept over him. Capture was inevitable.

'I'm done for!' he gasped, slumping miserably on to the seat.

The gypsy gave him an old-fashioned look. 'Friends of yours, I gather,' he said. 'Perhaps 'twould be best if you hid in the caravan.'

Jeremy jumped down from the driving seat, an easy matter since old Bess was scarcely going at more than a walking pace, and ran round to the back of the caravan where there was a neat little door. In a matter of seconds he was safely inside clutching his precious accounts book.

The interior of the gypsy's caravan was amazingly snug, though Jeremy had no time properly to appreciate it. Already he could hear the pounding of hooves, and as he crouched down out of sight of the windows he could hear them slacken from a gallop to a trot.

'Hello there, gypsy!' he heard Harrison Bradwell call.

'Good day to you, gentlemen,' the Romany replied. 'You appear to be riding hard.' He made no attempt to stop the trundling caravan.

'We are looking for a boy—a tall, dark-haired rascal,' said Harrison. 'Have you seen ought of such a lad?'

'Why do you seek him?' the gypsy demanded.

'Why? Because he burnt down Cressdale Mill, the young blackguard. There'll be a warrant out for him and there's a reward of five guineas for the man that catches the rogue.'

Hot blood flushed to Jeremy's face. He felt like springing from his cover and denying the charges there and then, but good sense prevailed. How could Harrison Bradwell of all people make such a charge? Jeremy felt a cold fury towards his enemy. He had another worry too—

a reward of five guineas was a tempting prize, and the gypsy was not a wealthy man.

'There was such a boy, I recall, back at the Tideswell cross-roads. He took the way to Castleton, I do believe,' the gypsy lied.

'Just as I expected!' Joshua Bradwell exclaimed. 'He's gooin' o'er t'Winnats, hopin' to throw us off scent! If we ride hard we'll catch him afore dusk!'

There was a clatter of hooves as the Bradwells turned their horses, and with cries of encouragement to the beasts, galloped off the way they had just come.

Jeremy sighed with relief and wiped a sleeve across his forehead.

'You can come out now,' he heard the gypsy call. 'They've gone.' The caravan halted.

Jeremy jumped out on to the road where he found the Romany dismounted and awaiting him, a grin on his handsome dark face.

'I cared not for your friends, young sir,' he said. 'As pretty a pair of villains as e'er I saw.'

'You saved my life,' Jeremy replied, 'and for that I am deeply grateful. They are wicked men and it's not true what they said—I didn't burn down the mill.'

The gypsy shrugged. 'What's one mill more or less?' he said. 'There's too many of them, as it is. But I would take the word of a boy I knew rather than that of those two men any day. Have you ever noticed how some people resemble animals? Well, the little man reminded me of a weasel and the big fellow had the mark of a jackal. Neither are pleasant animals, take my word.

'Like the jackal and the weasel, they are after easy prey— you. When they find you are not on the Castleton road after all, they will be back this way. Old Bess, here, I regret to say, has but one speed, as you may have noted, and they will soon catch up on me. You must go your own way.'

'But where will I go?' Jeremy asked. 'They are bound to find me.'

'Go where they are least likely to look, and that is the direction from whence they came—Castleton. If you cut across yonder low hills, keeping out of sight, you should evade capture. 'Twill be dusk in an hour or two.'

'Thank you for all you have done,' said Jeremy, warmly shaking the gypsy's hand.

'God speed,' replied the Romany. 'And I hope you find the justice you seek.'

A narrow track, which eventually petered out into nothing, led Jeremy towards the hills which separated him from the town of Castleton. Compared with the dark gritstone hills further north, these hills were mere hummocks of friendly limestone and short sweet grass. Nevertheless, they were steeper than Jeremy had first imagined and he was glad when his aching legs dragged him finally to the summit.

He was amazed at the way the landscape unfolded before him in the clear winter atmosphere. He could see for miles around and he readily identified Tideswell, Wardlow and the road to Castleton.

On this latter he could even discern the two Bradwells, looking like toy soldiers galloping along a narrow ribbon.

The Bradwells had obviously turned back from their wild goose chase and were heading once more for the main road to Chapel, where the tinker's caravan was making its snail-like progression. Other figures, too, had made an appearance on this highway and though he could not be sure at such a distance it seemed to Jeremy that it was Jem

Marsh and a group of apprentices. So they too were hunting him!

A sudden baying of hounds sent a chill down Jeremy's spine. The dogs from the mill! They were using the dogs to scent his trail! Already he could see that the animals were gathering around the very place where he had left the gypsy.

Jeremy turned and ran. How he ran! Desperately clutching the heavy book he stumbled across the hills as quickly as his legs would carry him. He jumped streams and scrambled over stone walls almost without pause. He ran until he could run no further, when his legs buckled beneath him and he fell gasping to the grass.

But the dogs had been running too, and were now much nearer.

Dragging himself to his feet he plunged on, black despair tearing at his heart. He knew full well that it was only a matter of time—that very soon the dogs would catch up with him.

It was just when he was on the point of collapse, when his legs felt like water, that he spotted the cave. It was nothing more than a small opening set high up in the face of a limestone escarpment, steep but not totally inaccessible to one as desperate as Jeremy. With his last grain of energy he flung himself at the rocks.

Once or twice he almost fell, as large pieces of rotten limestone broke away beneath his feet but at last he struggled into the cave and lay gasping on the cold floor. He had done all he could—the rest was in the lap of the gods.

He was none too soon. He had barely recovered his wind when the first of the dogs came barking over the last fold of hillside, followed by cursing and panting apprentices.

The dogs stopped at the foot of the cliff, yapping excitedly.

'He's scrambled up yon crag,' he heard Jem Marsh say. 'Happen it's a short cut.'

'Let's go round,' another voice replied. 'We have him trapped—he can't get far!'

Jeremy's heart sank. It was true enough, he *was* trapped. Sooner or later they would look in the cave.

It was dark in the cave. Feeling round with his free hand he could make out that the place was narrow but tall—he could not touch the roof. The walls felt cold and damp.

He decided to explore. After all, he had nothing to lose and with luck he might find another exit—one which would lead him to safety.

Progress in the cave was difficult. The floor was slippery with mud, sloping first one way and then the other, the walls, too, had a habit of jutting out in awkward places so that Jeremy was continually bumping into them. If only he could see! He felt like a blind man groping his way through a maze.

Suddenly and quite unexpectedly he came to a high vaulted chamber lit by a tiny hole in the roof. Jeremy was astounded. It was like being in some weird underground cathedral. Icicle-like pendants of white limestone hung from the ceiling or joined with others reaching up from the floor of the cave to form pillars. On the walls, limestone in all the hues of the rainbow, wet and gleaming eerily in the filtered light, was frozen into fantastic cascades. In the background like the bass notes of a church organ, he could hear the roar of underground water.

Jeremy had never seen anything like it before, and the beauty of it quietened for a moment his own anxieties.

Though the great cave had a hole in the ceiling, it was so innaccessible as to be useless as a means of escape, as Jeremy quickly realised. It was at least seventy feet from the floor to the roof and the sides of the cave were smooth and bulging.

He noticed, however, that the light was fading, that the winter daylight was turning to dusk. He must have been in the cave for an hour at least, and he had heard no sound of pursuit. Perhaps the dogs had led his enemies off on a false scent? The one certainty was that he could not remain forever in the cave, and dusk seemed a splendid time to escape.

He turned and groped his way back along the passage. It seemed worse than ever, and twice as long, but at last he caught sight of a glimmer ahead. He stumbled forwards —and found himself back in the great cave!

Only then did Jeremy realise that he was lost. What he had taken for a simple tunnel was in fact a labyrinth. The hill was like a honeycomb in which a man might wander for days, without finding his way out.

With a sense of panic rising in his throat, Jeremy turned and stumbled blindly back into the tunnels. This time he came upon a low roofed gallery, where he was forced to crouch almost double. He moved forward cautiously, feeling the walls with his free hand. Suddenly he sensed the roof going up again and he was able to stand upright. He took a step forwards. For a brief instance he was aware that there was nothing for his foot to rest on and he desperately tried to throw himself backwards, but too late.

He pitched forward into dark space and felt himself falling into a deep void. Suddenly with a sickening bump he hit a rock projection with his left side, tried to clutch at it, missed and fell again. He lost all consciousness.

CHAPTER EIGHT

CASTLETON

HE WAS DIMLY conscious of the tinkling sound of underground water, and of a numbing pain in his left side. He let out an involuntary groan, and to his surprise a deep voice said compassionately, 'Aw reet, young 'un. We'll hev thi out on here i' no time.'

Opening his eyes, Jeremy found himself in a rock chamber illuminated by the flickering light of a tallow candle. The roof of the chamber was low, so that the huge figure of the man bending over him was forced to kneel in the mud of the floor. He did not seem to mind, his only concern being for the limp figure of the boy.

Whether it was seeing someone after all his lonely experiences in the cave, or whether it was the kindly tone of the man's voice when he spoke, Jeremy was glad. Not that the man's appearance had anything about it to inspire confidence—on the contrary, the fellow looked like a brigand, with an ugly pock-marked countenance made more fearsome by an unkempt black beard, and a body so massive that he seemed to fill the little cave. His arms were like the branches of an oak, and equally brown and tough, and he had hands the size of shovels. His broad chest laid bare by an open shirt, was matted with hair and his rough canvas trousers, like those sailors wore, were held in place by a thick leather belt heavily studded with brass rivets.

But Jeremy cared nothing for the man's appearance—

he was too pleased to see him. 'Where am I?' asked Jeremy weakly.

'In one o' t'levels of t'Hurdlow Mine,' the man answered in a deep voice.

'Mine?' Jeremy cried, in surprise. 'A coal mine?'

The big man chuckled. 'Nay, lad—a *lead* mine. This country's full on 'em.'

Jeremy cringed as a spasm of pain went through his side.

'Tha's bruised thi ribs,' the big man said. 'It'll hurt thi a bit, but theer's nowt brasted.'

'I remember a big cave,' said Jeremy, 'and then I got lost in the tunnels.'

'Aye, that'd be t'Great Chamber,' the other explained. 'It's nobbut part on an underground system as runs for miles beneath these hills. Aw this land is hollow like a drum. A mon could wander in yon caverns and ne'er come out again!'

'But how did I get into this mine?' Jeremy asked, puzzled. 'And how did you find me?'

'Tha fell down an owd shaft. Tha sees, t'mines and t'caverns are really aw of a piece, meetin' and crossin' in aw sorts o' places. 'Tis not a shaft as we uses these times, but we keeps it open to let in air. Tha must hev fawed twenty feet—lucky for thee tha landed on deep soft mud!'

'I thought I was done for,' Jeremy confessed.

'An' so tha should a-been but for Lady Luck! No matter. Tha's safe now. Ah've sent mi sons for a litter, and we'll carry thi out.'

The journey out of the Hurdlow Mine on a canvas litter was not one that Jeremy wished to remember. The tunnels were narrow and dark, and though three more strapping

men turned up to help in the carry, and were obviously
the sons of the bearded giant, it was a long and agonising
business.

At last the cold sweet night air could be scented in the
tunnel and in another minute or two the rescue party
emerged into a dark and steep sided valley. Above him,
as he lay on the litter, Jeremy could see a clear purple sky
with a myriad stars glittering like diamonds.

Despite the darkness the men obviously knew the path
they were taking. Freed from the confines of the mine they
set up a cracking pace, down the narrow dale and into the
outskirts of a darkened village which Jeremy knew must
be Castleton. The houses were substantial dwellings built
of well dressed stone, and he could see the dark form of a
church against the night sky, but of inhabitants there was
no sign and he concluded that the hour must be very
late.

If he had expected to be taken to one of the houses,
Jeremy was quickly disillusioned. The stretcher party
marched across the village square then turned abruptly
up a narrow alley which led past some smaller cottages
and by the side of a rushing torrent. The alley became a
mere path and it quickly steepened into an uphill pull.
On either hand tall limestone cliffs began to close in until
it seemed to Jeremy that they were once more going into
the bowels of the earth.

And so they were. The path ran through a narrow
ravine into a cave, the like of which Jeremy had never
imagined possible.

The mouth of the cave was like the maw of some enormous rock monster. Inside, the floor had been shaped into
various level platforms, on two of which stood a group of
rude cottages. Strange figures flitted about in the flickering

light of a bonfire, and Jeremy was convinced now that the big man who had rescued him was indeed a brigand, and that this was the brigands' lair.

But he was past caring, he was so tired. The bearded giant seemed to sense this for he called for a bed of straw to be made up near the fire and they laid Jeremy on it and covered him with sheepskin rugs.

'Tha needs sleep, young 'un,' said the big man. 'And in t'mornin' there'll be time enough to discuss what's to be done wi' thee.'

When Jeremy awoke next morning he felt sore and stiff but otherwise in good spirits. He had escaped from Cressdale Mill! The realisation of freedom swept over him like a tide of joy, but it ebbed quickly enough when he remembered that he was now a hunted criminal.

The fire had burnt to low ashes and bright winter sunshine was streaming in through the open mouth of the cave. He lifted himself wearily from his couch and took a closer look at his strange surroundings.

The cave was even bigger than he imagined. It rose in a great vaulted arch fully sixty feet over his head and it was some two hundred feet wide and about the same in length, though the innermost recesses were in shadow and difficult to discern. The floor, composed of a mixture of earth and crushed limestone chippings, was divided into man-made levels which ran in parallel lines from the entrance to the rear. The cottages looked miserable affairs of an inferior type, constructed of rough hewn limestone with split flagstone roofs. Smoke curled from their chimneys to billow and blacken the limestone roof of the cave.

Some of the inhabitants were already about their work. They were a rough sort, dirty, unkempt and savage in looks, so that once again Jeremy was reminded of brigands.

One group in particular caught his interest. On one of the long, straight, platforms some men were stretching hanks of hemp between specially constructed metal plates. What they were doing was quite beyond Jeremy's imagination, and he regarded them curiously.

'Rope,' said a deep voice suddenly, from behind him. 'They're makkin' rope—same as they've done these past three hunnert year.'

Jeremy had been so preoccupied watching the rope makers that he had not noticed the approach of his rescuer of the previous night. He turned and found the big man smiling at him.

'Tha con caw me Big Amos,' said the man without formality. 'What's thi name, young 'un?'

'Jeremy Ollershaw, sir—and I have to thank you for rescuing me last night.'

'Well, Jeremy, tha seems to hev ketched no harm,' the giant replied. 'Though as for thi rescue—happen I saved thi for a wusser fate yet.'

Jeremy caught his breath. 'How is that, sir?' he demanded fearfully.

'Ah've been down i' Castleton this morn,' Big Amos explained. 'An it seems aw t'countryside is in a tizzy seekin' a young lad as burnt down Bradwell's mill at Cressdale yester-noon. Theer's a reward out—dead—or alive—an' folk are sayin' how 'tis a hangin' matter for sure.'

All the hardship and hunger which Jeremy had suffered during the last twenty-four hours seemed to assail him when he heard these words. He would have fallen had not Big Amos caught him.

'Howd on!' said the miner sympathetically. 'Tha's

noan etten for hours, I'll be bound. Tha mun hev summat
for t'ate, and tha con tell me aw about it. I reckons nowt
to being hung on an empty belly!'

Amos led him to one of the cottages, where he was soon
sitting on a stool at a freshly scrubbed deal table, ravenously devouring a huge bowl of stir pudding made with
fresh cream milk. This he followed by rashers of cold
boiled ham cut straight from the bone. Between mouthfuls
he explained to the miner everything that had happened
since the night he had arrived exhausted at Nook Hall:
how he had been cruelly apprenticed to Cressdale Mill,
and the wild riots which had led to the destruction of the
mill.

'But 'tis all useless,' he concluded, tears welling into
his eyes. 'They are bound to take me and who would
believe the word of a 'prentice lad against the Bradwells?'

'Happen so,' said Amos slowly. 'But tha forgettin' yon
accounts book.'

The words hit Jeremy like a hammer blow. Amos was
right! He *had* forgotten the accounts book! But where was
it? Had it not been lost in the Hurdlow Mine?

Amos set his mind at rest. 'Ah'm noan as daft as ah
look,' he said with a grin. 'Last neet, when we font thi
in t'mine, I asked misel' what were a young lad doin'
wanderin' in yon caves on a winter's neet? Why, I towd
misel'—he mun be a runaway 'prentice—they being ten
a penny in these parts. Ah! But I says, if he's runnin' away,
then why is he carryin' a damn great book?

' 'Twere a fair puzzle, wi' no immediate answer. Any-
road, when my lads browt thi here, I picked up t'book
from wheer it had fawd and fetched it along.

'And last neet, as thy slept, I went through yon book—
like ah towd thi, ah'm noan as daft as ah look!'

Jeremy felt a rising excitement. 'And when you had examined the books what did you find?' he asked.

'Same as thee—Harrison Bradwell's as twisted as yon rope outside!'

At that moment the door of the cottage burst open and a young man, well built and dressed in rough miner's clothes, stood on the threshold. He was out of breath through running.

'Fayther! Theer's a gang o' men marchin' up from t'village wi' Joshua Bradwell,' he announced. 'Ah reckons they've coom for t'young 'un!'

Big Amos sprang to his feet, a look of defiance on his face. 'Then they've coom i' vain,' he said. 'Quick, Jack, tha mun hide t'lad in t'cave.'

They hurried out of the cottage into the body of the cave, where the rope-makers had stopped work and were gathered in an angry band.

'We'll stop 'em, Amos!' cried a little old man, wrinkled like a walnut. 'We'll pelt 'em wi' rocks!'

'Aye!' chorused the rest. 'Down wi' tyranny!'

'Howd on, lads!' Amos cried with a voice of authority. 'Ah knows that tha's aw suffered from oppression, but it's noan thee that they're after this time—it's this young 'un. But they're noan goo-in' for t'find him. Jack here will tak him in t'cave, and we mun stop 'em from enterin'!'

'Follow me, lad,' said Jack. He led the way to the back of the cave where the daylight scarcely filtered. Here they came upon a small door, constructed of heavy timbers. Jack reached up to a ledge in the rocks and brought down a bundle containing some tallow candles and a tinder box. 'Howd these,' he commanded, thrusting the candles into Jeremy's hands. He busied himself with the flint and steel and soon the oily waste in the tinder box was burning.

Jeremy lit the candles and Jack carefully replaced the box on its shelf.

Beyond the door a narrow passage led into the bowels of the earth. The ceiling was low and the floor slippery with mud so that Jeremy found difficulty in maintaining his balance. Jack, however, being accustomed to work in a mine, found no difficulty and continually urged his companion to hurry.

At the bottom of the incline the tunnel widened into a sort of alcove, and by the flickering candle light Jeremy could see a dark pool of water stretching from wall to wall. All further progress seemed impossible, but on the pool was a small wooden boat, so crudely constructed that it was really nothing more than a floating box, or, as Jeremy thought with a shiver, a floating coffin.

'Do we go in that?' he demanded apprehensively.

'Aye—'tis safe enough, though it do leak a little,' Jack replied cheerfully. 'We mun pass through a tunnel i' t'rock. Lie down an' keep thi candle on thi chest. Theer's nobbut just headroom.'

Jeremy scrambled into the boat and lay down as he was bid on the wet planks of the floor. He felt faintly unnerved lying there, staring at the limestone roof as it reflected the light of his candle.

Jack lowered himself into the water by the boat. It was deep—up to his armpits—and cold, though he seemed not to notice it. He had laid his candle aside and now he began to push the boat towards a low black hole at the far side of the pool.

Jeremy could see nothing of this. He was only conscious that the boat was moving. Suddenly, the limestone closed in like a trap: the boat bumped gently from side to side of the tunnel and the roof came lower and lower until it was within an inch or two of his upturned face. A panic-like feeling of claustrophobia gripped Jeremy and he felt like jumping up to escape the pressing rock walls, but he knew that he had to keep a tight control over himself. Gritting his teeth, he watched the roof skim overhead.

The journey seemed like an eternity, though in fact it lasted scarcely more than a minute or two. It ended dramatically—the roof and walls simply melted away into the darkness and the feeling of oppression gave way to a sense of vast cavernous space. The boat crunched gently on to a gravelly beach.

'Where is this awful place?' he asked as he helped Jack to pull the boat on to the beach. It seemed like an eternal void, his single candle failing utterly to reveal either walls or roof.

'Folks caw this t'Devil's Chamber,' his companion replied, and seeing how Jeremy shuddered, he gave a laugh which echoed and rang from huge invisible walls and soaring vaultings. 'Hev no fear, young 'un,' he added philosophically. 'Better the devils in here than them as waits for thee out yonder!'

'What would you have me do?' Jeremy asked, setting a brave face on matters.

'Wait here, until ah cooms back for thi. It met be hafe an hour, happen longer—it aw depends on how fayther is tacklin' Owd Bradwell and his cronies. One thing's for sure—they'll noan get thi in here!'

At the entrance to Peak Cavern, Big Amos stood with legs astride and his massive hairy arms akimbo, staring down the track to the village. Behind him, their faces full of determination, ranged his sons and the rope-makers. Persecution was nothing new to them. They lived strange lives in their great cave, and were half feared, half hated by the villagers. They resented any intrusion into their private little world.

Amos himself had grown up the son of a rope-worker but his adventurous spirit and sharp intelligence had led him to explore his native hills and turned his thoughts to mining. Miners had a status accorded to no other class of person in the High Peak; rights and privileges which went back for centuries and which made them a powerful group, almost beyond the grasp of ordinary laws. Amos had been fortunate: he had found and claimed the Hurdlow Mine, as was his right, and it had made him passing wealthy despite his working clothes. However, he had never forsaken the rope-workers amongst whom he had been brought up.

To them he had extended the umbrella of protection created by his being a free miner, and they in their turn readily acknowledged him as their leader. Had he been a villain or a greedy man there is no doubt that he could have done great harm in the area, for he controlled what was virtually a small army of twenty men or so, everyone of whom would have died for him, but Big Amos wanted nothing except to see that none of his poor brethren starved and that everyone, whether rich or poor, should have justice.

It was raining hard. The bare black trees dripped water into a thousand rivulets and the steep walls of the gorge beyond the cave were streaked with the velvet of oozing moss. A bend in the path hid the village from sight, but Amos knew the Bradwells could not be far away.

He did not have long to wait. A noisy rabble, headed by Joshua Bradwell and his son came toiling up the stony track. They were armed with pitchforks, muskets and plain wooden staves and as they struggled upwards they laughed and joked as if they were on a noisy picnic. Some were apprentices and overseers from the burnt out mill, others farm hands and villagers, out for the excitement of a man hunt and the chance of a five guineas' reward.

They constituted a ragged assembly whose appearance had not been improved by the rain, and the two Bradwells were no better than the rest. What with fighting the fire and then hunting Jeremy over the moors their clothes were stained and torn and their hands and faces grimy.

They had taken no time out for niceties such as washing or shaving. The night they had spent in a barn and they had greeted the morning rain with foul tempers, which had mollified somewhat when news reached them that a boy had been found in the Hurdlow Mine. The Bradwells had no doubt as to who that boy would be. Their search for Jeremy was at an end.

Big Amos watched them approach. He disliked the Bradwells and all their type; mean, grasping, cruel employers who grew fat from the hardships of young apprentices; men who had seized upon the scientific marvels of God and turned them into instruments of the Devil. It gave him grim satisfaction to see them wet and bedraggled.

'How then, Josh Bradwell!' he called, when the invading band were within easy earshot. 'What brings thee to Peak Cavern, and what means aw these armed men?'

The Bradwells came to halt, and their followers gathered into a silent band.

'I hears tha's getten a 'prentice o' mine,' Joshua replied. 'Yon lad tha font last neet i' Hurdlow.'

'Happen,' Amos said, non-committally.

'Then be so good as to hand him o'er. He's a desperate

young villain and 'tis fitting he be brought to justice!'

'Is this what tha caws justice?' Amos sneered, indicating the mob. 'Seems a rough sort o' justice to me!'

' 'Tis the sort he deserves!' cried Harrison Bradwell, angrily. 'The rascal burnt down Cressdale Mill, and by mi' faith, we'll turn him off for it!'

'Aye!' cried the mob. 'Hang the villain!'

Harrison stepped forward until he was face to face with Amos. 'You see how matters stand,' he said threateningly. 'These honest men have hunted young Ollershaw all night, and they do not intend to be robbed of their prey. Nor do I.'

Amos looked at him with smouldering eyes and a face set like hewn granite. There was something in the look which warned Harrison of danger and he took a hasty step back.

'Aye, tha'd best step back, Mester Harrison,' said Amos calmly. 'Or happen I'd tak thi apart wi' mi bare honds!'

Harrison stepped back further.

'Tha not talkin' wi' one o' thi miserable hafe-starved 'prentices now,' Amos continued. 'Ah'm a free miner, an' tha knows as well as onybody, that what ah says here is *law*. Or would tha like to dispute it wi' a Bar Coort?'

The mob had heard these last words and shuffled uncomfortably. Nobody in his right mind wanted to fall foul of the Miners' Court.

Joshua Bradwell got the message, too, and he hurriedly tried to make amends for his son's behaviour.

'Tak no notice o' t'lad, Amos,' he said, in a conciliatory tone. 'He's out o' sorts this morn—but tha sees our problem? Yon Jeremy Ollershaw is bound 'prentice to me, and 'tis my duty to look after him. Tha mun hand him o'er.'

5

'Now that's wheer tha wrong,' replied Amos with a grin. '*If* the lad is here—and ah'm noan admittin' owt—then tha mon find him.'

Joshua hesitated but Harrison cried, 'Let's search the cave!'

'Aye!' cried the mob surging forward.

But out of the shadows came the rope-workers, to form a solid, grimly determined barrier across the mouth of the cavern. Amos grinned even broader, his white teeth gleaming against his dark bushy beard.

'Well now,' he said, almost apologetically. 'It seems as if my neighbours object to thi tramplin' aw o'er their homes. Between thee and me, Joshua, ah con tell thi that they're good lads at heart, but a mite rough wi' strangers. There'll be a few cracked pates afore tha gets in here!'

Joshua Bradwell could see who held the whip hand. His evil eyes glinted. 'Ah'd heerd tha was a damned Revolutionary,' he said. 'Tha'll pay for this! 'Tis a matter for t'Law.'

' 'Tis a matter for *justice*,' Amos corrected him. 'Which may not be t'same thing. Ah bids thee good-day, Joshua Bradwell!'

Left alone in the Devil's Chamber, Jeremy set about exploring the place, not so much out of curiosity but from a feeling that the activity might take his mind off the awful loneliness. It was like being abandoned in a black tomb: cut off from humanity and hope. Even the Hurdlow Mine with its labyrinthine tunnels had not felt so lonely—then he had at least the thoughts of escape to distract him.

The light from his candle made scarcely an impression on the utter darkness of the cavern. He was able to see a few feet ahead, and no more, but by careful footwork he managed to gauge the immense size of the place, and he was intrigued to discover that on one side there was a steep slope of fallen boulders, like scree down a mountain-side. It looked as though in some long gone past, one wall of the cave had collapsed, or perhaps some upper cavern had fallen into this lower one.

For the want of better to do, Jeremy began climbing the boulder slope. Up and up he mounted, with loose stones rattling below his feet, but he seemed to get no nearer to the roof, which remained invisible. At last, tiring of the exertion, he picked his way down again.

As he neared the foot of the boulders he caught sight of a curious reflection from his candle on the floor of the cave. It made him start, for it gave the floor the appearance of a gigantic mirror. Eager to know what could cause such a phenomenon Jeremy scrambled down the remaining boulders to discover that the entire floor of the cave was covered in water!

He could hardly believe his senses. Only ten minutes ago he had been standing on that same floor—a floor made of gravel and limestone. Now it was covered in water, and quite deep too—he tested it and found it came up to his knees.

Even as he watched he saw the edge of black water creep further up the boulder slope. The cave was flooding, and he was trapped inside it!

Inch by inch the rising waters forced him back up the boulders. He wondered desperately how high the water could rise—surely it could not fill a cavern as immense as this? But then he recalled how clean and polished all the rocks had appeared, even those on the boulder slope, and how there had been no limestone stalactites such as one should find in a cave like this, and he realised with a quick

flash of intuition that continuous ebbing and flowing of
water would lead to conditions such as these.

He felt a rising sense of panic. He was trapped, and
there was absolutely nothing he could do about it.

Suddenly there was a vigorous thrashing of water and
a head and shoulders appeared on the dark surface of the
pool.

'Amos! Amos!' Jeremy cried, almost sobbing with relief.

'Howd on, lad!' came the miner's strong voice, full
of reassurance. In a few seconds he had hauled himself on
to the boulders, where he knelt for a moment, gasping for
breath.

'Praise be tha's aw reet!' he gasped fervently. 'Ah thowt
tha mun be drownt, for sure.'

'I found these boulders,' Jeremy explained. 'But what's
happening? Why is the cave flooding?'

' 'Tis raining Heaven's hardest out yon,' said Amos,
'and theer's been a lot o' rain o' late. This chamber acts
like a well for aw t'watter that cooms down—an' it
con fill i' ten minutes! Lucky for thee it's noan so fast this
time—but theer's noan tellin' when it met quicken so we'd
best be out on here fast!'

'But how?' cried Jeremy.

'Same road as I came in—through t'tunnel.'

'But it's under water—we'll drown!'

'Happen so—but 'tis certain we'll drown if we stays
here.'

Jeremy looked at the big miner. He could see the iron
determination on the man's face and he realised that Amos
had already risked his life in coming to rescue him. He
couldn't let Amos down—and though he felt very much
afraid, he tried not to show it.

'Let us go quickly,' he said.

Amos permitted himself one of his rare grins. 'Good lad!' he said. 'Howd thi candle and follow me.'

Together they waded into the cold waters of the dark pool, now up to Jeremy's armpits. Amos led the way towards the far wall of blank, smooth limestone, knowing exactly where the tunnel lay, even though it was totally submerged.

'Reet,' the miner said. 'Us lives depend on gettin' through fust go. One mistake, an' we're done for.'

'I understand,' said Jeremy.

'Good. Theer's nowt to be afeared on provided tha keeps a cool yead. Tak howd on mi belt—got it? Then keep a tight grip. Tha mun follow me at aw speed, for we'll noan be lingerin'. Dowse thi candle.'

Jeremy let the candle fall into the water. It went out with a quick hiss, leaving them in total oppressive darkness.

'Reet lad—tak a deep breath an' howd it. *Now!*'

Jeremy felt the icy waters close over his head and funnel into his ears. He kept a tight grip on Amos's belt and found himself dragged along under the water at incredible speed so that it was all he could do to keep his feet. Once or twice he cannoned into hard rock, but he scarcely noticed it. His lungs ached and ached until he felt he was going to burst and he went suddenly lightheaded . . .

'Aw reet, lad,' said Big Amos, as Jeremy came to his senses again and discovered himself lying on firm ground. 'We've getten through!'

CHAPTER NINE

AT THE KING'S HEAD

DESPITE A COLD east wind coming off the moors as a reminder that winter was not yet completely gone, there was a considerable crowd of idlers gathered outside the *King's Head* at Chapel en le Frith. Word had gone round that on this day the Justices were to hear the case against Jeremy Ollershaw, already notorious as the lad who had burnt down Cressdale Mill.

The story had lost nothing in the retelling. There were those who thought that Jeremy was a French spy sent over by the Revolutionary Government to cause havoc in British cotton mills, and they pointed to the strange way in which he had first made his appearance at Nook Hall, to his dark skin and his 'foreign' way of speaking. Others, taking the lad's part, ridiculed the spy story by maintaining that Jeremy was too young for a spy, and that the fire was an accident caused by the riot at the mill. But whether they were for or against him, they were all agreed that he had caused a memorable sensation.

In the tap room of the inn, Peter Bramwell, the parish sexton, gave his own views to an admiring audience.

' 'Tis more than just a lad burnin' down a mill,' he said, with a gravity becoming his profession. 'Theer's been mills burnt down afore an' like as not theer'll be mills burnt down again. But yon's different. Mark my words!'

Just why it should be different he did not make clear, but the others in the crowded room agreed with his senti-

.ments and banging their pewter tankards on the tables, roared for more ale. A tousled haired pot-boy wearing a dirty apron made his appearance.

'Hev t'Justices arrived as yet?' Bramwell demanded.

'Nay, Mester Bramwell,' said the boy. 'Though I doubt they'll be long. Room's aw ready for yon.'

In fact, the room had been ready since the previous evening, for although the Justices often used the *King's Head* for their meetings, the landlord had on this occasion gone to some trouble to match the general excitement. He had prepared a special parlour, normally reserved for overnight guests, as a courtroom, with three high-backed arm-chairs for the Justices and settles for everyone else. It was not a large room, but it was well lighted by modern windows of the sash type, to compensate for the dark wainscotting and heavy oak beams. A table, supplied with quill, ink and paper stood between the Justices' chairs and the rest.

Jeremy was the first to arrive, driven in a hired carriage from Castleton and well guarded by Big Amos and his sons. The crowd at the inn door greeted them with a mixture of cheers and boos, but Amos ignored them and gently ushered Jeremy inside.

Amos had been busy ever since the visit of Bradwell to the Peak Cavern. He knew that whatever hardships Jeremy had suffered at the Cressdale Mill, the law was firmly on the side of Bradwell. Jeremy was an indentured apprentice, whether he liked it or not, and as such, Bradwell was legally entitled to claim him. But that was not the same as saying that Jeremy had set fire to the mill— and Big Amos believed the boy implicitly when he said that Harrison was the culprit in that affair. The falsified accounts book was valuable supporting evidence to this.

It had been Amos's decision to bring the whole matter into the open before the Justices at Chapel en le Frith. If he could prove that Jeremy was innocent of the charge of arson and at the same time indict Harrison Bradwell—well, there was a slender hope of getting Jeremy free. It was a chance, but one which had to be taken.

Once his mind was made up, Amos worked quickly. He used his considerable local influence to get the Justices to hold a special meeting at the *King's Head*, and it had come as a complete surprise to the Bradwells when they received a summons to attend.

'Ah doan't like this,' was old Joshua's comment to his son when he first heard of the court. 'Theer's summat i' t'wind. Amos knows summat, tha con be sure—an' it'll bode nowt good for us. Why else bring Ollershaw to court?'

'But he *can't* know,' said Harrison. 'Nobody but you and I know that Ollershaw . . .'

'Howd thi tongue!' his father cried sharply. 'Least said an' soonest mended!'

The Bradwells, with Jem Marsh, followed closely behind Jeremy's party. Joshua nodded coldly towards Big Amos who gave him a contemptuous look in return, but the two parties did not speak to one another. They sat at opposite sides of the room, conversing among themselves in low whispers.

Shortly after the Bradwells, came Sam Ollershaw and Betsy. Sam, looking nervous, wore his best breeches and jacket of sober blue—a suit he reserved for funerals—but Betsy wore a pretty dress and a gay pink bonnet which tied under her chin with a long satin ribbon. When Jeremy saw them he sprang to his feet and rushed forward. Betsy threw her arms around him, kissed him and hugged him, tears of joy running down her cheeks. For a moment neither spoke but then Betsy, realising that there were other people present and watching them with amused glances, broke away and said shyly, 'I'm reet glad to see thee again, Jeremy.'

'And I to see you, Betsy,' he replied. 'I thought of you often and longed to be at Nook Hall.'

He turned to Sam, who stood there grinning happily. They clasped hands in warm friendship. The soft hearted farmer was as near to tears as pride would allow, and to tell the truth, so was Jeremy.

'How art keepin', lad?' Sam said in a low voice.

'The better for seeing you, Sam,' Jeremy replied. 'But where is Martha? She's not taken ill?'

'Nay, her's noan sick, lad,' said Sam. 'Her's getten important business in Chapel and her'll be along soon. It *must* be important to miss seein' thee, I reckon—her's fretted mightily since tha went away.'

But the mystery of Martha's absence was not discussed, for at that moment the doors opened to admit the Justices of the Peace.

Just what Jeremy had expected he wasn't sure—impressive figures in robes and full bottomed wigs, perhaps, looking like noble lords, but the reality was much more sober. Two of them were obviously prosperous local farmers, dressed in neat broadcloth suits. They were brown from an outdoor life and spare of build, and so alike that they might have been brothers. The third Justice, however, was totally different. He was short, of portly build and wore a pale blue suit of a rather old-fashioned cut, stained with snuff and ale marks. His face was round and red, his wig too small, and only his eyes denoted a shrewdness a casual observer might miss.

'Who's that?' Jeremy whispered to Sam.

5*

'Sam Bagshawe of Ford Hall,' the farmer answered. 'He's the squire—an' he's noan the fool he looks.'

The Justices took their appointed places with Bagshawe seating himself, as if by rights, in the centre chair. The Clerk, the same little man who had taken Jeremy to Cressdale, fussed around, arranging the paper and quills. Gradually the room filled with spectators from the tap-room, noisily carrying on their conversations, and, so it seemed to Jeremy, totally oblivious of the solemnity of the occasion.

At last the Clerk called for quiet. 'This Court is con-vened in order to examine—' he began.

'Aye, aye! We know all about that!' boomed the deep voice of the squire. ' 'Tis likely to be a long dry meeting, I'm thinking. Landlord, fetch the Justices some ale, and thee, lad—' he pointed a fat forefinger at Jeremy and gave him a stern look, 'get on thy feet and let's be having thy tale.'

'I protest!' cried Harrison Bradwell, springing up. 'That brat's the one who is on trial and 'tis not right he should speak first!'

Samuel Bagshawe opened his eyes wide at this unseemly interruption. 'When I wants thy advice, sirrah, I'll ask for it,' he said heavily. 'As far as I'm aware *nobody* is on trial—this is an examination to obtain the facts, and no more. You'll get your say in due course—but until such time, pray allow *me* to conduct the proceedings!'

Harrison sat down, scowling. Jeremy began his tale, uncertainly, hesitating and with a weak voice, but as he went on he recalled the horrors of Cressdale Mill and this lent him more determination. Not that Sam Bagshawe seemed to be paying the slightest attention: the ale had arrived and after taking a good pull at it, he unbuttoned his waistcoat, eased himself back in his chair and gave every appearance of falling asleep.

Jeremy had just finished telling how he came to Nook Hall, and was about to relate his adventures at Cressdale when the squire cocked one eye open and said, 'So your real name is not Ollershaw, eh, lad? Who are ye then?'

'That I cannot tell, sir,' replied Jeremy. 'The coach accident caused me to lose my memory so completely that I have no knowledge of my origins.'

'Humph!' said the Justice. 'Remember the accident quite well. Shockin' affair. Shockin'.' His finger pointed suddenly at Sam. 'This correct, Ollershaw? Is it as the lad says?'

'Aye, sir,' answered Sam. 'He just turnt up one neet, hafe deed from cowd and famine. He must hev walked Rushup Edge and stumbled on Nook Haw by accident.'

'And there was nowt to say who he was or where he came from?'

'Nowt, sir.'

Bagshawe nodded, as though everything was now much clearer.

'Very well,' he said. 'Sit thee down, lad.'

'But, sir!' Jeremy protested. ' 'Tis the mill I want to tell about . . .'

The Justice sighed wearily. 'I do wish people would let me conduct this hearing in my own way,' he said in exasperation. 'I know all about how you became an apprentice at Cressdale Mill—what I want to hear from Mr Bradwell is how the mill came to be burnt down.'

Joshua Bradwell rose to his feet. 'Ah con tell thi what ah knows,' he said, 'but 'tis best towd by my son Harrison who was more immediately concerned. But this much ah will say—yon brat has been nowt but trouble sin he came to Cressdale. He run away once afore, tha knows.'

Bagshawe looked sternly at Jeremy. 'Is this true?' he demanded.

'Aye, sir, but . . .'

'That's not good, lad. Not good at all. Indentures are legal bonds meant to be honoured. I take a poor view of your conduct. However, we'll hear what Master Harrison has to say.'

Harrison rose lazily to his feet. He was dressed in his best London clothes of plum coloured jacket and knee breeches, with a striped lemon waistcoat of silk.

'There had been some minor trouble in the mill yard,' he drawled. 'A young apprentice had been insolent, and whilst I was chastising him, he ran off. Unfortunately he fell into the mill race and was drowned.'

Unable to endure this travesty of the truth, Jeremy sprang to his feet. 'That's a lie!' he shouted. 'You murdered Joey!'

Harrison turned on him, livid, 'Hold your tongue, brat!'

Sam Bagshawe brought down his fist with a crash on the table which made the inkpot jump. His face was stern and anger flashed momentarily in his eyes.

'Enough of that!' he commanded. 'We'll conduct this hearing without turning it into a tavern brawl! Ollershaw —if you interrupt again, I'll have you committed without more ado, so help me! Continue with your story, Bradwell.'

'As I was saying, the boy was drowned. Unfortunately, there were many apprentices present, including Ollershaw. As my father has already told you, sir, this Ollershaw was ever ready to make mischief and he used the accident to start a riot. The apprentices ran wild, smashing furniture and machinery, destroying their very livelihood, the ungrateful devils, and all the time urged on by Ollershaw. Then Ollershaw disappeared and shortly after that the mill began to burn.'

Sam Bagshawe held up a hand to stop him.

'One moment,' he said. 'Did anyone actually *see* Ollershaw set fire to the mill?'

Harrison shrugged his elegant shoulders. 'Who else could it be?' he demanded. 'Ollershaw was the only person not accounted for—and if it were not he, then why did he run away? Innocent people don't run away.'

'That's true,' the Justice reflected. He gave Jeremy a black look and the boy's heart sank. Things were not going too well.

'We followed him for a day and a night across the moors,' Harrison continued. 'My father and I endured severe hardships but we persisted because we were determined to bring the young scoundrel to justice. Eventually we ran him to earth in the Peak Cavern, where the miners refused to give him up.'

Sam Bagshawe pushed back his wig as Harrison finished.

'Can anyone substantiate this extraordinary story?' he demanded.

'My father, of course, but there is also Jem Marsh, one of the mill overseers and a most estimable person—he will bear out all I say.'

Big Amos had listened to Harrison's lying testimony with growing concern. Things were looking black for Jeremy. At the mention of Jem Marsh's name, however, he had a sudden idea. He was a judge of a man, and he knew Marsh's type well enough: bully and coward—the two often went together. As the Justice was finishing with Harrison, Amos went over to where Marsh was standing.

'It's thy turn next, Jem,' Amos said quietly.

The overseer gave him a wary glance.

'Whatever yon scoundrel Harrison has put thi up to, just thee remember one thing,' Amos continued. '*We hev t'accounts book from t'mill!*'

It was a shot in the dark but Amos had the satisfaction of seeing it strike home. A look of fear flickered in Marsh's eyes, showing that he realised the gravity of Harrison's lies, and that he might be accessory to some crime he knew nothing about.

In fact, had Amos but known it, Jem Marsh was a very worried man. Though he had half promised the Bradwells to help them with their testimony against Jeremy, he still had a shrewd suspicion that he might be paddling in deep waters. Who was the Ollershaw boy? Why were the Bradwells so down on him? There were too many unknowns for Jem Marsh's tastes and as he rose to give evidence his mind was in a turmoil of conflicting loyalties.

'Now, Marsh,' the Justice said. 'Tell us what you know of this affair.'

'Ah knows nowt,' he replied sulkily. 'Ah was workin' betimes.'

Bagshawe did not much like this reply. 'Come, sirrah!' he said sharply. 'Are you trying to say that the mill where you worked had a riot and was burnt to the ground, and you saw *nothing*? By mi faith, but if you don't speak I'll have you committed for contempt!'

'Ah was workin' at t'hoist,' Marsh said, sullenly. 'It were towards t'end o' dinner time. Theer was a crowd i't yard arguin' wi Mester Harrison.'

'Did you see young Ollershaw in the crowd?'

Marsh licked his lips nervously. 'No, sir,' he replied.

Harrison Bradwell sprang to his feet in a fury. 'You

demmed liar,' he shouted. 'Tell them how Ollershaw roused the mob!'

The room became a babble of excitement at this unexpected development until Bagshawe once more restored order by hammering on the table with his massive fist.

'By my oath!' he shouted. 'I'll have every one of ye committed to Derby Assize for rioting! Now then, Marsh, do I take it that Jeremy Ollershaw was *not* in the crowd?'

'He were wi me at t'hoist!'

Bagshawe looked sternly at the fuming Harrison Bradwell.

'And what do you reply to that? Master Bradwell,' he demanded.

'The man's a liar!'

'But we have your own word for it that he is a most reliable witness,' said Bagshawe acidly. Turning to Marsh he said, 'What happened then?'

'When Ollershaw saw Joe Walls faw into yon mill-race he give a cry o' distress an' rushed down to t'yard. He were very font o' Little Joey—they was comrades—and from where I was standin' by t'hoist, ah seed Ollershaw go dashin' down to t'river bank as if searchin' for Joey's body.'

A short rustle of excitement from the crowd was quelled at once by a stern glance from Bagshawe. 'Now let us get this aright,' said the Justice. 'If Ollershaw was with you when the other apprentice was drowned he could not have started the riot, could he? Furthermore, if he then went down to the stream, he could not have taken part in the riot at all, and therefore could not have started the fire. This is most puzzling. You realise that your evidence contradicts everything that Master Bradwell has said?'

'Mester Harrison towd thee what he *thinks*,' replied Marsh truculently. 'Ah towd thee what ah *saw*.'

'Then who *did* start the fire?' asked the puzzled Justice.

'He did!' Jeremy sprang up and pointed an accusing finger at Harrison Bradwell. 'He burnt the mill down in the hope of destroying *this*.' And he held aloft the heavy accounts book.

When Harrison Bradwell saw the book he gave a shriek like a demented being and rushed across the room to try and grab it. But he had not reckoned with Amos and his sons. Arms like steel traps clamped around him and he was held fast, kicking and struggling. The room was in pandemonium.

Bagshawe banged the table so hard that the inkpot flew off altogether and the contents splashed the dark floorboards, but even so it was some minutes before order could be restored. Amos's sons had kicked Harrison's feet from under him and now held him captive by the simple expedient of sitting on his chest.

'Silence!' roared Bagshawe for the tenth time, and by a miracle, a hush descended on the room. 'That's a sight better,' he continued. 'My God! I'll have the whole of Chapel transported to the Colonies if there be another disturbance! Now, boy, what is this book that causes so much uproar?'

But it was Joshua Bradwell who replied, not Jeremy. The mill owner had suddenly become a pathetic figure, aged and crumpled. He knew well enough what the accounts book meant.

'Yon's the mill accounts,' he said in a low voice. 'Ollershaw were given t'job of addin' 'em up.'

'You let a 'prentice add your accounts?' demanded Bagshawe in some surprise.

'Ah'm noan a one for figures,' replied the mill owner flatly. 'Harrison does the accounts, but for some while now ah've suspected they were being altered. Ah give Ollershaw the job o' checkin' 'em.'

Jeremy took up the tale. 'And I discovered that Harrison had been falsifying the accounts and stealing money from the mill! Unfortunately, before I could tell anyone, the riot started and Harrison, spying his chance, set fire to the mill hoping to destroy any evidence. At the same time it offered a chance of throwing the blame on to me, so that if I said he had been embezzling money nobody would believe me—they would say I was making it up out of spite. But what Harrison did not know was that I managed to rescue the accounts book!'

'Amazing! Quite amazing!' exclaimed Bagshawe. 'This clears you of the charge completely, young man, though as for *him*,' and he pointed at the prostrate Harrison, ' 'tis quite another matter.' He addressed himself sternly to Joshua Bradwell. 'I must tell thee, Joshua Bradwell, that if ye prefer charges against your son, and those charges are proved at the Assize Court, things will go badly for him. 'Twill mean transportation at the very least, and possibly worse.'

'He's still my son,' said Joshua sadly. 'Theer's no charges.'

'So be it. But he has seriously misled us here today with false evidence and for that I'm going to bind thee over to see that he keeps the peace henceforth or I'll send him for trial on a perjury charge.'

'He's nobbut a young fool,' said Joshua bitterly. 'He'll noan do it agen!'

'Then there is nothing more to say, and we can conclude this meeting,' said Bagshawe with obvious satisfaction.

'Sit thi down, Sam Bagshawe, tha's noan done yet!'

The court turned in surprise. The door from the tap-room had opened to admit Martha Ollershaw, and with her a remarkably wizened old woman, dressed in fine black velvet with her grey hair covered by a lace shawl. Her body was frail and bent, her bony hands grasped two silver headed canes for support. Her face was brown and wrinkled like a walnut, but her eyes held a black brilliance which was startling in one so ancient.

She hobbled through the silent courtroom until she came to Jeremy. Her black eyes looked into his face keenly and then, as if she had decided something, she nodded abruptly. 'This the lad, Martha?' she demanded.

'Aye, that 'tis! Oh, Jeremy! How art thi lad?' And he fell into her arms and for the first time in many days, sobbed.

But the attention of the crowd was riveted on the old woman in the black dress. She seemed to hypnotise them and there was no doubt that they were all afraid of her. As she hobbled forward towards the Justices' table there was no sound except the rustling of her voluminous dress and tapping of her sticks on the bare boards.

'Tha knows me weel enough, Sam Bagshawe,' she announced, fixing the squire of Ford Hall with her sharp eyes. 'Folks caws me Owd Becca, the Witch o' Chapel.'

'Indeed, madam, I have the honour,' Bagshawe stammered. 'But I fail to see why . . .'

She rapped her stick on the table for him to be silent and his voice trailed away to a halt.

'Then tha should know that ah ne'er leaves my house fro' one year's end to t'next, except on very important affairs. *This* is very important—or ah'd noan bother for t'come! Ah've getten summat for t'tell thi concernin' yon lad.'

The Justice nodded. He was no fool. Becca was a woman of considerable importance. For as long as anyone could remember she had been known as the Witch of Chapel and the locals held her in awe and sometimes fear because of her supposedly magic powers. Not that she had ever harmed a soul; her reputation rested on her soothsaying, which had been remarkably successful, compounded as it was from an intimate knowledge of everything that happened locally, a prodigious memory and a shrewd brain. Her fame had spread far beyond the confines of her native village, and it was not unknown for titled ladies from as far away as London to pay her visits for the purpose of seeing what the future held for them.

Over the years she had amassed considerable wealth from her fortune telling and had put the money to good use, buying property as far afield as Manchester. Though she herself lived in a humble cottage as she had done all her life, she could have bought Ford Hall quite easily, had it been for sale. She was not a person to be lightly put aside.

'When yon lad stumbled on to Nook Hall an' was cared for by Martha Ollershaw, it were t'first piece o' good luck he'd had for mony a day,' she began. 'Martha's no fool— around t'lad's neck she font this talisman. Tak a good look at it, Sam Bagshawe, and tell us what tha sees.'

She handed to the Justice the silver disc which Martha had found hanging round Jeremy's neck when he first came to Nook Hall.

'It bears an engraving,' Bagshawe said, examining it closely. 'Three stars, 'twould seem.'

'Aye—and what does that signify?' Old Becca demanded, eyes bright.

Bagshawe was frowning as he gazed at the medallion,

as though trying to recall some distant memory. 'It stirs the memory,' he admitted. 'But what it is—wait though! I have it now! This is the crest of the Hope family. But the line died out years ago, surely, with old Sir Geoffrey Hope?'

'Ah! But that's wheer tha wrong,' said Becca, with relish. 'Owd Sir Geoffrey had a son—Ralph Hope—who left these shores for t'Indies o'er thirty year ago.'

'I remember now!' Bagshawe exclaimed. 'There was some scandal—Ralph Hope killed a man in a duel and was forced to flee the country. But nothing more was ever heard of him—surely he must be dead?'

'Oh, aye, he's deed reet enough—but only last year. I recognized the talisman at once. It has been in the Hope family for generations, and is used as the personal insignia of the eldest son of the family—Lady Hope once showed it me when her paid me a visit. Of course, it went to the Indies wi' Ralph.'

Sam Bagshawe nodded comprehension. 'In that case,' he said slowly, 'this young man must be Ralph Hope's son!'

Whilst Old Becca had been speaking Jeremy's mind was in a whirl. At the mention of the Hopes he had suddenly found his mind filled with half-remembered, half-forgotten scenes of tall palm trees, blue skies and blackamoors. He could hear the rumble of surf on wide beaches and the natives' plaintive chanting as they stooped to pick indigo. Slowly it all came back to him.

'It is true!' he blurted out aloud. 'My memory is coming back and I remember who I am! My name is Geoffrey Hope, son of Ralph and Mary Hope of High Lea Plantation in Jamaica Island. My parents died of the fever last year—how long ago that seems now! The plantation was sold and the slaves dispersed, and with my old nurse and my father's manservant I was sent back to England to my grandparents' home in Derbyshire.'

'Aye, that has the ring o' truth,' said Old Becca. 'Though thi fayther would not know that his parents had been dead for mony a year, and t' estate brokken up. It would be thi nurse and t'servant who died in t'coach crash o'er Winnats Pass.'

Big Amos who, like everyone else in the crowded room, had been following the story with keen interest suddenly gave a great bellow of laughter. 'Tha's a free mon, now, young 'un!' he cried.

But Joshua Bradwell protested, his face very angry. 'Don't assume too much!' he cried. 'Ah've still getten his indentures—he's still a 'prentice!'

But Amos laughed even louder. 'That's noan reet, Mester Bradwell,' he said. 'Them indentures are in t'name o' Jeremy Ollershaw—but this young mon is Geoffrey Hope!'

Sam Bagshawe agreed. 'He's right. The indentures are invalid and no longer binding.'

Bradwell's countenance was twisted with hate and fury but there was nothing he could do to alter matters. 'Ah've had enough o' this tom-foolery!' he cried in rage. 'Kindly let that rascally son o' mine get up off t'floor—we're goo-in wom.'

'Tha noan goo-in afore everyone present hears t'story of tha villainy, ye black-hearted devil!' said Old Becca with unexpected vehemence.

Bradwell paled. 'Ah'm noan afraid o' thee ...' he blustered.

'Then tell 'em why tha wanted yon lad as a 'prentice in t'fust place—or happen I'd best tell it.'

'Go to the Devil!' cried Bradwell, trying to force his way out. But Big Amos and Peter Bramwell, the sexton, barred his way. 'Happen tha'd best stay,' said the sexton, pointedly.

'Aw this trouble stems fro' the greed an' avarice o' one mon—Joshua Bradwell. Years ago when t'new machinery began to mak cotton folk prosperous, Joshua Bradwell seed his opportunity for t'mak a fortune. He had a bit o' brass put bye an' his credit were good for moor—enough for t'start a mill, onyroad. Aw he needed were land for t'build on.

'But land were noan easy for t'coom by. At last, after a lot o' arguin' he persuaded owd Sir Geoffrey Hope to lease him a piece o' land at Cressdale—Cressdale Manor bein' part o' t'Hope estates for generations back, as tha knows. He would liked to hev bowt it, but Sir Geoffrey wouldn't sell. Aw that Joshua could get were a short lease. He took it 'cos he could get nowt else, an' every day he waited meant money lost.

'Well, Cressdale Mill were prosperous—it made Joshua a lot o' brass. But aw the time he had this short lease hangin' o'er him like a noose. Every year t'mill grew moor prosperous—*an' every year t'lease grew shorter.*

'Then Sir Geoffrey deed. There seemed to be no heirs: Ralph Hope had vanished, and it were like as not that the estate would be brokken up.'

Sam Bagshawe thumped the table in surprise. 'By George!' he exclaimed. 'In that case Bradwell could buy the land!'

'Aye, and at a cheap price. For who wants land wi' a mill on it except t'mill owner?'

'Is that the way of it, Joshua Bradwell?' Bagshawe demanded.

'Aye!' cried the mill owner defiantly. 'It's aw very well for thee to talk, Sam Bagshawe—thee wi' aw thi acres o' land and fine house. But ah built up Cressdale Mill from nothin'. My fayther were a drunken labourer on a farm an' he set me to work at the age o' seven. Well, ah worked reet enough—and ah scrimped and saved every penny until ah become an overseer at Dick Arkwright's mill at Cromford and finally ah had enough put by to start Cressdale.

'That owd miser Sir Geoffrey wouldn't part wi his land and ah could see t'day coomin' when ah'd hev to quit Cressdale—throw away aw ah slaved for! Then he deed, an' ah thowt ah were saved.

'But one day i'Chapel, Harrison seed this lad—an' there were no mistakkin' his features. He's a Hope all o'er—tha's only getten for t'look at his dark skin an' his face to see that.

'When Harrison towd me about him, ah made enquiries —an t'rest tha knows.'

Sam Bagshawe looked grave. 'Indeed we do,' he said sombrely. 'Finding that the lad had lost his memory you had him bound apprentice so that he could be in your charge where there would be little hope of him ever discovering his true identity. To protect your own selfish interests you were prepared to sacrifice this lad's inheritance and good name. I find this despicable beyond words, sirrah!

'Fortunately for you, this is not a court of assize, nor are you on trial, else I warrant that you would be made to suffer.' He pointed to Harrison, still held on the floor. 'Perhaps that's your punishment: a waster for a son! We have a saying hereabouts I doubt not you well know— *Rags to rags in three generations*—and that I fear will be the fate of the Bradwells! And now take your wretched son, and clear out of Chapel, for by Heaven there's none here will speak to either of you again!'

Outside the *King's Head* a pale spring sunshine lit the honey-coloured stone of the old street and brought the first warmth of the year to the moorland village.

Jeremy stood outside the inn, arm in arm with Betsy, looking at the ancient village with renewed interest and hope. A great load had been lifted from his young heart, and all his terrible experiences had not been in vain. He knew now the meaning of freedom, and it had been worth the struggle.

'It all looks so different now,' he said. 'There was a time when I hated this country, but not now.'

'Aye,' Sam Ollershaw agreed, 'it maks a difference reet enough. Tha's passin' rich now lad. Theer's not mony as is a 'prentice one minute an' a mester next!'

'But I don't want to be a master!' Jeremy cried angrily.

'What dust tha want?' Sam asked.

'I want to learn how to build dry stone walls that won't fall down, and to gather the sheep off Brown Knoll, and how to fix a barn roof . . .'

Sam grinned. 'But for aw that, lad, tha'd hev to live wi' us at Nook Hall,' he said.

'Sam Ollershaw thas a reet gubbins!' exclaimed Martha joyously. 'Isn't that what t'lad was sayin' aw along?'

BACKGROUND TO A STORY

BACKGROUND TO A STORY

JEREMY OLLERSHAW LIVED in an age when England was a very different place from what it is today. In some ways it was much more beautiful; towns were smaller, villages more isolated and there were wide tracts of open country completely unblemished by ugly lines of electricity pylons or the odorous fumes of trucks and cars. Even the railway was a thing of the future, and the few canals scarcely affected the scene at all.

But the change had started, as the gypsy told Jeremy, you may remember. The Black Country already earned its name, and steam was beginning to oust natural water as the provider of energy for factories and mills.

The early mills, set in little valleys at the foot of the Pennines, were often quite attractive to look at and some of them remain so to this day. Perhaps one day you will be able to take a stroll along Miller's Dale in Derbyshire and see for yourself Litton Mill and Cressbrook Mill nestling beneath the limestone crags, and I am sure you will agree that it seems incredible that these lovely old mills were once the scenes of some of the worst child-cruelties ever perpetrated. If you know the area, it will come as no surprise that the Cressdale Mill where Jeremy served his apprenticeship is the Cressbrook Mill of Miller's Dale.

But though we may regret the passing of rural England, we have good reason to rejoice that we did not live in those days. By our present day standards, the customs of the people, rich and poor, were generally barbaric; fighting, gambling, drunkenness were commonplace, and robbery with violence was not one bit lessened by the harsh laws. Many quite minor offences were punishable by death.

As to standards of comfort, there was a great gulf between the rich and poor. The wealthy landowners, often families who could trace their ancestry back to the Norman Conquest, lived up to their lordly status, with great castles or country mansions staffed by dozens of servants. Almost as rich (and sometimes even richer) were the new industrialists: men who had seized on new inventions and turned them to profit, like Sir Richard Arkwright, who owned several mills in Derbyshire. These men, and the comfortably well off country squires like Samuel Bagshawe of Ford, owned practically everything; they were the classes from which came the powerful Justices of the Peace—who were amazingly successful at keeping districts under control.

Craftsmen of all sorts flourished too, and for many people times were not so bad insofar as they had a warm cottage, clothes and plenty of food and drink, but there was also a great mass of the labouring classes for whom existence was a terrible struggle. There was no Welfare State in those times, of course, and if a man failed to provide for his family, then they starved. Hours of work were long, factory conditions appalling and a man could be dismissed on the spot, for no offence whatever. If a man went sick, then the family might well find itself in difficult circumstances.

Perhaps one of the most horrifying aspects of life in those days was the way in which children—and very young children—were brutally treated. There were schools of various sorts, from the great boarding schools like Eton and Rugby, to local grammar schools consisting of perhaps a dozen pupils and a master, as well as more elementary 'schools' devoted to the three R's, but if they existed today in the form they then had, the Ministry of Education would promptly close them down, and probably send the Governors to prison as well! Most children had no formal education of any sort; they were put to work at the earliest opportunity.

Children, particularly of the labouring classes, were brutally treated at home, and they expected no better at work. Worst of all were the poor apprentices; a name which had become a mockery in Jeremy's day.

The apprenticeship system, by which a boy was indentured to a master craftsman in order to learn his trade, had worked well for many centuries. When the mills came along, with their need for lots of cheap labour, the mill owners saw in the apprenticeship system a ready-made source of free workers: in return for teaching a child the craft of spinning (which they seldom did) the boy or girl was 'bound' to the owner until his or her twenty-first birthday. Since many of the children were only seven years old at the time their indentures were signed, it meant fourteen years of virtual slavery. The conditions which Jeremy endured at Cressdale were by no means exceptional, and though there were one or two more enlightened and humane employers, others were far worse— so many children died at Litton Mill, for example, that the owner was ashamed to bury them in the churchyard and had them buried out of the parish.

You may well wonder where all the children came from. Some, incredible though it may seem, were actually indentured by their own parents, but the majority were orphans from the various Poor Law institutions, particularly in London. The trouble was that each parish was obliged to look after its own poor, including orphans and abandoned children, and this could cost a lot of money. The Parish Officers, anxious to save on rates, indentured the children simply to get rid of the expense of keeping them.

Of course, right from the start there were good and honest citizens who cried out against this traffic in human lives. One of them was a mill owner himself, Sir Robert Peel, but the fight for justice was a long and bitter one as you can find out from your history books.

Whenever I read a historical novel I always find great pleasure in visiting the places mentioned, though some-times it is years before I can do so—half the pleasure of walking along Bagworthy Water is to imagine that the fierce Doones are still in their lair, and what would Rannoch Moor be without memories of *Kidnapped*? The scenes of Jeremy's exploits are certainly worth visiting, and I promise you that it is very exciting to see the Peak Cavern where Amos lived, and where the rope-walks still exist—though I regret to say that the boat journey through the tunnel is no longer necessary because a passage was cut to allow Queen Victoria to visit the cave!

Telford drove a new road into Castleton from Chapel en le Frith, but it is still possible to motor along the Winnats Pass, to see the startling limestone crags and to look at the great cone of Mam Tor. Like Jeremy, too, you can escape from the world along beautiful Ravensdale and climb to the top of Peter's Stone.

If you want to identify Nook Hall with Slack Hall, well, who am I to argue? Certainly you will find Ford Hall where the Bagshawes lived until quite recently and of course, a much enlarged Chapel en le Frith, which calls itself The Capital of the Peak, and where the Bramwells still provide the sextons for the village church as they have done for centuries.

In fact, you can still visit all the places that Jeremy knew, with the exception, I regret to say, of the grand old inns. That is where he has the advantage over you—nowadays, the police take a very poor view of anyone under eighteen years of age walking into a public bar and demanding a pint of ale! However, if you do visit Derbyshire I am sure that your father will be quite willing to testify that the *King's Head*, the *Devonshire Arms* and the *Bull's Head* are as hospitable as ever they were in days gone by!